SUSPICION

SUSPICION

SORCERY AND SECRETS™
BOOK TWO

RIVER TATUM

MICHAEL ANDERLE

DON'T MISS OUR NEW RELEASES

Join the Florid Romance email list to be notified of new releases and special promotions (which happen often) by following this link:

https://floridromance.lmbpn.com/about/sign-up-for-our-newsletter/

Published by Florid Romance
an imprint of LMBPN Publishing
2375 E. Tropicana Avenue, Suite 8-305
Las Vegas, Nevada 89119 USA

Version 1.00, March 2025
eBook ISBN: 979-8-89354-577-7
Print ISBN: 979-8-89354-578-4

ONE

Cassandra rose just after daybreak, waking to a chill that seeped through the shutters and into her small chamber. The keep's atmosphere felt different this morning, thick with anticipation, a quiet but disturbing hum she could sense along her skin. She had slept fitfully, haunted by images of strange runes flickering in unlit corridors, and by the memory of Taron's labored breathing when his aura almost slipped from his grasp days earlier.

After shrugging on a fresh gown of serviceable gray linen—no finery for her, not even in Baron Ulric's halls—she secured the protective talisman Miriana had given her around her neck. She didn't need a mirror to know she was a bit of a mess--her hair was loosely braided, a few strands escaping to frame her face. Exhaustion pressed behind her eyes, but she refused to let herself appear fragile in a keep rife with suspicion.

Beneath her door, a thin line of light revealed that the corridor was already awake with passing guards and servants. A single guard lingered today, shifting on his feet by her threshold. She recognized him: Jareth, one of those assigned to watch her during the night. His expression was carefully neutral, pretending he was simply on ordinary duty and not posted to ensure she didn't leave her room unattended.

"Morning," Cassandra said tersely, stepping out and pushing the door closed behind her. "Is there a summons from the baron already?"

He dipped his head. "Not yet, mistress. But...there have been...rumblings." With that vague response, he kept his gaze averted. She guessed he had no more details. Or if he did, the fear of Ulric's wrath kept him silent.

She made no answer, only inclined her head and headed through the corridor's weaving passages. At every corner, she sensed curiosity hovering. Maids paused in their tasks to stare. Two stewards parted like startled birds as she approached, hush-cradling their words behind raised hands. Before, their censure had pricked her nerves and incited anger.

Now, she saw the shape of their gossip and realized it had grown sharper overnight. The sabotage overshadowing Taron's warding posts, small but relentless hints that someone tampered with them, had now snowballed into a monstrous rumor that Cassandra herself was the saboteur. She clenched her teeth, pushing down the wave of frustration.

She thought of Taron's confession, how he'd revealed the lengths his father had gone to keep him silent about her exile. Anger for all the lost years mingled with an unwilling empathy for Taron's battered conscience. More than once, she'd awakened from restless dreams with the echo of his voice in her mind, remembering how he had looked at her, equal parts contrition and longing. Now, dawn had come and brought a more immediate problem: forging alliances in a keep where nearly everyone stood ready to blame her the moment another ward fell apart.

At the turn leading to the ground-floor corridor, Sir Barro stood waiting. A strong-jawed knight with stoic brown eyes, he'd been one of the first to show even cautious faith in her. He still looked wary, he was, by nature, a cautious man, but he had come to see that her wards healed more than they harmed. Days ago, she had swiftly tended a guard who'd been caught tumbling from a vantage point near Taron's corridor, a minor incident overshadowed by swirling sabotage. That intervention had softened Sir Barro's suspicion.

"Good morning," Cassandra said, approaching him. She kept her voice low. There were so many ears that could be listening in these halls.

He crossed his arms, glancing around for prying eyes, then inclined his head. "I'd hoped to catch you before the day's bustle." His tone carried caution, but also a hint of urgency. "We've discovered something new in the archives."

Her pulse beat faster. "Show me."

He jerked his chin for her to follow, leading her down a side stairwell that wound toward the keep's lower level. Three turns later, they emerged at a narrower passage with fewer torches, only the occasional tapered candle set in a wall sconce. The archives spanned a series of connected rooms that smelled of ancient parchment and old dust. As they neared the stout wooden door, Cassandra caught a glimpse of a clerk scurrying out with an armful of scrolls, eyes flicking her way in alarm.

Sir Barro pushed the door open. "He's inside," was all he said. Cassandra guessed he meant Taron.

Indeed, Taron stood near a table crowded with ledgers and half-unfurled records. His shoulders tensed the moment she entered, and when he turned, the lamplight deepened the tired half-circles under his hazel eyes. A static charge seemed to cling to the air around him, as if his volatile power had not fully settled from past surges.

"Cassandra." There was faint tension in his voice. He was wearing a fitted, dark-blue tunic embroidered with subdued runic lines near the cuffs, presumably to help regulate mild fluctuations. Sweat dotted his temple, suggesting he might have already wrestled with some lesser surge this morning.

"Sir Barro said there's new evidence," she prompted, stepping closer. She took note of the quill and the black pot of ink perched precariously atop a tall ledger. Another ledger lay open, revealing lines of painstaking text. Sentries hovered, presumably lower-ranking knights or clerks, their expressions torn between suspicion and curiosity.

Taron nodded. "We've found...a suspicious entry from late last night." His gaze flicked down to a page with carefully scribed details. "It logs additional requests for warding materials, rune-carved rods specifically.

According to this, you," he paused meaningfully, "signed for them."

Even though she had anticipated it, a bolt of anger lanced through her. "I never touched those rods. Nor did I sign for them."

"I know," Taron murmured. "But this signature is alarmingly similar to your own scrawl, whoever forged it is skilled at mimicry."

She leaned over to look more closely at the page. In the low lamplight, she saw the careful loops of script, shaped to resemble her own measured cursive. A jot of frustration stabbed her chest. "I see they even used the slight flourish I make on the final stroke of my name." Her tone tightened. "No wonder half the keep thinks I'm tampering with the wards. This is thorough."

Her mind raced. If someone was planting these requests, it would appear that she'd frequently visited the archives or storerooms to withdraw runic supplies after hours. Bile churned in her stomach at how meticulously they were framing her. First a rumor, then these false ledgers. The sabotage scheme was escalating.

Taron's left hand twitched, a visible spark dancing across his knuckles. He took a slow breath, then pressed his palm flat on the table's edge, likely grounding himself as she'd taught him. "Whoever is behind this," he said softly, "they're waiting for the next slip-up to cry foul about you. We can't let that happen."

"I've told you," Cassandra replied, voice low, "my wards would never sabotage your magic. I want to keep it from destroying you." She shook her head. "It's exhausting, always being the first suspect."

He opened his mouth, perhaps to offer reassurance, but a hush fell as Sir Barro cleared his throat from the door. "I've posted a guard to track any further nighttime sign-outs," the knight said. "But if the forger is cunning, they'll find another way."

A swelling roar of frustration filled Cassandra's chest. Still, she forced herself to keep her composure, an outburst might only feed the rumors about witches being volatile. Slowly, she exhaled. "Thank you, Sir Barro. Let's continue to gather evidence quietly. The moment we can prove these sign-outs are forged, we might corner the real culprit."

Taron brushed a knuckle across his forehead, wiping away a bead of sweat. "My father is summoning the council in about an hour to discuss morning affairs. He'll expect us there. He's likely to demand results, or to use the sabotage as a way to corner you."

"Then we'll be ready," she said, though her heart pounded.

They parted ways. Sir Barro accompanied Taron, presumably to intercept any suspicious ledger runners, while Cassandra made for the corridor that led back to the keep's main floors. The tapestry-lined halls swarmed with heightened activity: pages carrying messages, knights hustling with expressions of faint alarm, and a swirl of maids whispering behind their hands. Word of the forged ledgers might already be out, or another rumor might have woven itself into the keep's fabric.

Cassandra felt those hushed stares like pinpricks against her back.

She paused at a small alcove near a window. A jagged sliver of the morning sun cut across the stone floor, illuminating swirling dust motes. Taron's father had forced her return, demanded she anchor Taron's surges, and now allowed these rumors to take root. But she couldn't back down. Lives in the barony were at stake, Taron's included. Summoning a deep breath, she steeled herself and continued on.

THE COUNCIL CHAMBER was filled with voices even before Cassandra stepped through the tall double doors. At least a dozen individuals were present, lords, stewards, scribes. The central table gleamed beneath the light of tall candelabras, and along the walls, more watchers hovered: lesser knights, a scattering of local notables, and a cluster of anxious officials. Large windows on the far side let in pale daylight, though the chamber's fine tapestries and heavy drapery gave the space a dreamlike gloom.

She tried to keep her shoulders squared, ignoring the hush that rippled through the room as she entered. Taron was already there, standing near the far end of the table. Baron Ulric, enthroned at the table's head like a self-appointed king, turned to look at her with penetrating scrutiny. He wore a dark, formal doublet embroidered with the baronial crest, and his graying hair swept back from a face etched by lines of control. Cassandra stiffened, feeling the old anger coil in her belly whenever she met Ulric's gaze, he had shattered her life once, threatening far worse if Taron disobeyed him.

"Mistress Cassandra," Baron Ulric said, in a voice filled with cold politeness. "We were just discussing the... unrest." He let the final word hang, as though labeling Taron's precarious aura and all the sabotage as a single entity.

Cassandra inclined her head toward him in greeting. "My lord."

Ulric's gaze flicked to the seat near Taron, a silent order that she take it. She complied out of sheer necessity. Taron nodded at her, a minute, private gesture of support. She caught the faint lines of tension bracketing his mouth, as though he, too, dreaded what Ulric might do next. His eyes met hers briefly, and in their depths she read both resolve and bitterness. Despite the open space between them, Cassandra felt a telling thrumming in her chest at his presence.

TWO

A steward was already speaking from the opposite side of the table, recounting an incident from the night before in which one of the outer wards flickered strangely. Cassandra listened with mounting suspicion. Could the saboteur have tested a partial rune shift, enough to cause Taron's wards to falter?

"...the farmland posts near the orchard shimmered," the steward explained, voice halting, "though no full breach was detected. A guard swore he saw a figure in a cloak vanish into the orchard. Yet we have no proof. No footprints were found."

The mention of cloaked figures had become distressingly common. Knuckles tightening on her lap, Cassandra forced her tone to remain level. "There seems to be a pattern. Saboteurs appear briefly, tamper with wards, then vanish without a trace." She glanced pointedly at Ulric. "It would help if we increased watch rotations at night."

Before Ulric could respond, Taron spoke up. "I concur," he said, voice firm. "We can't dismiss these incidents as coincidences any longer. If we truly want to protect the farmland, and ensure my magic doesn't slip into another surge, someone needs to guard those warding posts."

Ulric's mouth flattened. A muscle ticked in his jaw. "If we reassign more knights to night patrol, the keep's interior might be undermanned, particularly given your... precarious condition." His gaze darted to Taron's wrist cuff, and by extension to Cassandra, who had helped craft additional wards on it.

A section at the table shifted, revealing a few counselors eyeing Cassandra, tension evident in their stances. One of them, an older noble with thinning hair, coughed gently. "These illusions of sabotage might simply be the product of Mistress Cassandra's... unusual powers," he remarked, so cordial as to be insulting. "We can't discount that magical interference might be more direct on her part."

Cassandra clenched her teeth. She'd expected it, but hearing these half-veiled accusations stung. She inhaled, remembering Taron's confession, remembering the guard she'd aided. She forced a calm tone. "I have done nothing to harm the barony. The notion that I would sabotage Taron's wards, which I'm here to stabilize, makes no logical sense."

Baron Ulric steepled his fingers, fixing her with an unreadable stare. "Logic and witchcraft do not always align, do they?"

Cassandra's cheeks burned. Taron stiffened, fists

curling atop the table. She sensed the old intimidation tactic: get her riled, make her snap, so her anger might smear her reputation even more. But she refused to let Ulric see her fury in raw form.

"Given the rumors that someone has forged my signature on supply ledgers," she said, projecting calm, "I'm inclined to believe that these illusions, if illusions they are, serve someone else's agenda."

A ripple of interest crossed the watchers. She glimpsed a flash of agreement in Sir Barro's eyes from behind the smaller cluster of knights. Good. She needed that support.

Ulric eyed her. "Show us these... forged ledgers. Have you concrete proof or just speculation?"

Taron's voice sharpened. "We do have a ledger, Father. I saw it myself this morning. The scrawl is nearly identical to Cassandra's signature, signed out for runic rods at an impossible hour."

"And do you bring it forward to present?" Ulric's tone was all barbed courtesy.

"I have it," Sir Barro interjected, stepping up. He carried a small sheaf of pages, carefully folded under one arm. "Only this one, but there are likely more. We'll continue our search. If you examine the detail, my lord, you'll see the hour recorded was well past midnight, and Mistress Cassandra was nowhere near the archives then."

Ulric flicked his gaze over the parchment, a sculpted frown forming. For several heartbeats, he said nothing, analyzing the page. Across the table, another counselor peered with wide eyes, then whispered something to a companion.

At length, Ulric set the sheet down. "A convincing attempt," he conceded. "But it could also be that a cunning witch might attempt to disown her own record." His voice was deceptively mild, though the threat in it tingled across Cassandra's ears.

She realized with chilling clarity that he would neither confirm nor deny her innocence, he was simply planting more doubt. A wave of resentment rolled through her. She nearly spoke, but from the corner of her eye, she saw Taron's knuckles whiten as he clenched his fists.

In a measured breath, he said, "Father, continuing to cast suspicion on Cassandra when we have mounting evidence of outside tampering only helps our enemies. If the saboteur remains free to manipulate the wards, or my aura's stability, the consequences could be catastrophic."

An uneasy pause followed. Cassandra could feel tension ratchet around the table, a physical thing. Some men avoided looking her way, as if uncertain whether to believe her claims or indulge the baron's implied doubts. Others studied her openly, curiosity in their eyes, no doubt seeing the flush of anger in her cheeks.

Eventually Ulric's mouth thinned. "Very well," he said at length, turning to a scribe. "Keep searching. For the moment, we will assume the possibility of forgery and step up guard rotations, though that, too, might strain our resources." He looked back at Cassandra. "Meanwhile, you will demonstrate 'effective results' in anchoring my son's wards. I want to see fewer talk of surges, fewer rumors that Taron is on the cusp of meltdown. Understood?"

Cassandra's hands tensed in her lap. She carefully

drew a breath. "As am I, so I will continue reinforcing them daily." She forced a polite tone. "But sabotage remains likely... my lord." The title tasted bitter on her tongue.

From his seat at the far side, Taron remained silent. He was clearly swallowing his frustration. She stole a glance at him, and their gazes met in momentary accord. A swirl of heat flared beneath her ribs, that old mixture of longing, anger, and complicated gratitude for his recent defenses of her.

Ulric sniffed and turned away, dismissing her with a gesture. "If that is settled, we have other matters to address."

The baron launched into a secondary topic about the farmland's finances, a routine affair overshadowed by the tension in the room. Cassandra let the words wash over her, conscious that even as Ulric spoke, more eyes flicked to her. She noticed Sir Barro standing guard-like near the table. Taron folded his arms, posture rigid. She guessed he was doing his best not to let his father's barbs ignite another surge.

When the council finally ended, Cassandra stood on shaky legs. She had managed to sit quietly through the baron's official pronouncements, giving the minimal courtesy demanded of her. Now, the lords were dispersing, each heading off to duties or private gossip. Ulric lingered only for a moment, exchanging clipped words with another noble. Taron muttered a curt excuse to a steward, then strode toward Cassandra.

She saw the turbulence in his eyes the moment he

reached her side. "I'm sorry," he breathed, voice low enough not to carry beyond her. "I wanted to say more, but if I pressed, Father would only use it to further undermine us." His gaze flicked over her face. "He's determined to keep suspicion swirling. I hate it."

A hundred retorts rose in Cassandra's mind. She forced them down, focusing on the swirl of conflicting emotions that always beset her at times like this. "He's an expert at manipulation," she said quietly. "Don't apologize for failing to best him in one council meeting. The sabotage is bigger than just his fancy words."

His jaw tightened. "That's exactly what I'm worried about. The forging of your signature makes it clear the saboteur has resources, access to official ledgers, the ability to falsify your script. We need to track them down."

She nodded. "We do. And soon."

For a moment, they stood in the council chamber's corner, half-hidden by a tall tapestry depicting the barony's crest. Taron's aura felt alive, a subtle pulse that she recognized after so many times anchoring him. He breathed in, stepping fractionally closer so the hem of his tunic brushed the edge of her gown. There, in that too-intimate space, she could smell the faint tang of ozone that always clung to him after a flare. She recalled the tremor in his body during those moments she pressed her palm to his chest to siphon off the chaos.

"You're exhausted," Taron murmured, his tone gone quieter. "I see it in your eyes. Have you slept at all?"

She exhaled. "Little. Every time I do, I dream of tampered wards, or I jolt awake thinking someone's at my door with another accusation." She offered a tight smile. "But it's no worse than living in exile, if I'm honest. At least here I can try to fix what might otherwise bring the barony down."

He studied her with a haunted expression, as if her reference to exile reignited old guilt. Then he lifted a hand slightly, as if he wanted to touch her cheek. But remembering all the watchful gazes, he let his arm fall. "We'll find the culprit," he said softly. "And no matter what else, I won't let him, or anyone, destroy you again."

Her heartbeat jolted. She felt the weight of the confession he had made before, how he had wanted to protect her back then but found himself blackmailed into silence. That vulnerability in his eyes struck her. Despite the anger that still simmered, she gently nodded, acknowledging his vow. She wanted to trust him. Maybe she already did, more than she would ever admit to the baron or the rumor-hungry halls of this keep.

Sir Barro approached, effectively breaking the moment. "Lord Taron. Mistress Cassandra," he greeted in a clipped tone. "We should compare notes about last night's orchard incident. Perhaps see if those footprints connect with the forged ledger's date."

"Agreed," Taron said, stepping back from her. "Lead on."

They left the chamber as a group, ignoring the prying looks from the few bystanders lingering near the door. Cassandra, still unsettled by the near-intimacy of Taron's presence, forced her mind to the practical matter of orchard patrol schedules.

THREE

The next few hours passed in a blur, filled with a whirlwind of frantic activity. Cassandra and Taron poured over the orchard guard logs, cross-referencing them with times recorded in the archives' sign-out registers. Sir Barro enlisted two other knights, both men who had begun shifting their suspicion away from Cassandra ever since the sabotage became too blatant to blame on a single witch.

Their quiet watchfulness hinted at acceptance, or at least caution in labeling her as the culprit. She gleaned from their hushed asides that they respected how she had stepped in repeatedly to anchor Taron's surges, preventing harm to the keep's staff.

Between scouring half-burned records in the library and verifying storeroom entries, Cassandra felt the ache of mental exhaustion. In a dust-choked corner behind a row of old crates, Taron found traces of runic symbols etched in chalk, symbols not part of any official barony protection. A shivering, half-finished pattern that looked suspiciously like something designed to unravel wards. They recognized it quickly for what it was: sabotage in midcrafting.

By midafternoon, her throat felt parched, and her eyes burned from pouring over ledgers that listed wards and runic rods. Meets the orchard sabotage time. The same ledger that pinned blame on her also cross-referenced the orchard wards. A subtle pattern emerged: each forged request timed closely to the tampering outside. The correlation was enough to suggest that while Cassandra was "signing out" rods, Taron's wards out by the orchard were being manipulated. A perfect setup to slander her.

They documented it all. Taron scribbled notes, and Sir Barro gathered statements from guards. By now, a few of those guards had personally seen scuffed footprints, even glimpsed cloaked silhouettes darting away in the orchard's predawn gloom. Cassandra pinned each shred of evidence to the overarching puzzle. A sabotage plot. The conspirators wanted Taron's wards to fail. Either they intended to let his magic tear him, and possibly the barony, apart, or to let Cassandra take the blame for undermining him.

At one point, Cassandra rubbed her temples, leaning against a tall shelf in an obscure corner of the keep's library archive. "This is bigger than we realized," she said softly, her voice echoing off the dusty spines of ancient tomes. "Someone with high-level access is systematically forging these records and messing with wards outside. They have resources."

Taron stood close, concern lining his face. "We suspected as much," he said. "My father might even suspect it, but I doubt he'll show all his cards. He's too intent on scapegoating you if it means controlling the narrative." His gaze flickered with frustration. "I want to defy him openly, but... you saw how easily he twisted everything at the council this morning."

Her pulse quickened, recalling the razor-edged moment with Ulric's cynicism. "We don't have enough proof to accuse any single individual," she said. "And while we wait to gather more, the real culprit is out there, forging more signatures and tampering with wards. We could race in circles for weeks."

"Yes," Taron said, half under his breath. "But we can't stop. Even piecemeal evidence might eventually corner them." He raked his fingers through his hair, looking worn. "And in the meantime, I have to keep my aura in check. If sabotage intensifies, the surges might get worse. I, " He shot her a conflicted look. "I hate putting you through that, Cassandra."

She swallowed. "Don't. It's nowhere near as terrible as letting you burn yourself out." She paused, forcing a faint, wry smile. "Not to mention we might burn half the castle if your magic tears the wards wide open."

A whisper of a smile ghosted his lips, though it didn't fully reach his eyes. "I suppose you're right." He exhaled, tension shaking his shoulders. "Thank you."

Those two words carried more weight than she was prepared for. So she simply nodded, feeling an unspoken warmth pass between them. The air between them felt charged, fragile, as if the smallest word or gesture might shatter it. She opened her mouth to respond, but the steady echo of Sir Barro's footsteps on the library's stone floor broke the moment.

She turned toward the sound, her heart sinking just a little at the interruption, though she quickly masked it with a composed expression. The knight's presence was a reminder of the world outside this quiet exchange, one where neither of them had the luxury of staying vulnerable for long.

"I have news," the knight said in a hushed voice. A flicker of urgency crossed his face. "A clerk overheard talk from a steward who mentioned your name again, Mistress Cassandra, and not kindly. He says you've requesting a brand-new brand of runic chalk from the storeroom." Barro's mouth curled with grim irony. "We both know that's a lie."

Her entire body tensed. "Did the steward say when I supposedly made the request?"

"Just this past hour," Barro said. "And obviously you've been here all along. I demanded he show me the sign-out slip. He claims it's locked in a scribe's desk for now."

"Locked away so no one can question it," Taron murmured, eyes narrowed. "They're not even trying to hide the forgeries at this point; they're just stockpiling 'evidence' so they can unleash it when it's most advantageous."

Cassandra felt her throat tighten. "This is relentless." Fear twisted inside her: the knowledge that if enough official records stacked up against her, no matter how ridiculous, the baron would have a public excuse to condemn her. She could practically hear the false accusations: She's untrustworthy, she orchestrated sabotage. The thought made her chest seize with something akin to rage.

Sir Barro nodded, concern etched in his face. "I'll do what I can to keep that slip from being turned into official condemnation. But my reach only goes so far among the stewards."

He nodded and left. For a long moment, Cassandra and Taron were alone in the hush of the library. She became acutely aware of how closely they stood, hidden from prying eyes by the tall shelves. The hush pulsed with tension, her frustration at these schemes, Taron's smoldering anger at his father's manipulations, and a more intimate current she both yearned for and feared.

"Taron," she managed softly. "If Ulric or any of these conspirators attempt to bring me down, I need you to focus on what matters, your safety, the barony's stability. You can't let them turn your aura into a weapon."

He looked at her as though her words wounded him. "I won't let them do this to you," he said. "Not again. I was silent once. Not now."

His quiet vehemence made her breath a hitch. She recalled every lonely night in exile, cursing him for that silence. Now, confronted with his heartfelt determination, she wanted so badly to trust in the vow. It pulled at her heart, tangling with the pain of the past.

She mustered a shaky breath. "All right," she whispered. "Then help me gather the last bits of proof we need.

So many nights I've lain awake, hating this place. But if there's a chance we can unravel the sabotage, maybe turn this barony away from the worst, I have to try."

Nodding, Taron hesitated, then lightly touched the back of her hand with his fingers. The contact was brief but electric, sending a ripple of unspoken comfort through her. After an instant, he withdrew, as though scalded by the knowledge that if they lingered in each other's space too openly, it might spark more rumors. She sensed his magical aura stir in subtle arcs, responding to the closeness.

CHAPTER

FOUR

Without another word, they left the library, returning to the labyrinth of corridors where the day's final hours pressed on them with suffocating intensity. Whispers followed in their wake, overshadowing the last of the sunlight streaming through the arrow-slit windows. The keep's gloom deepened, and the hush of onlookers fed Cassandra's simmering fury.

Rumors coiled like serpents in every hallway. Yet she squared her shoulders, determined to press on, ignoring the mistrustful eyes. By dusk, they had compiled a rough timeline: each false sign-out in the ledger coincided with a reported "accident" or glimmer of tampering. Lined up, it formed a suspicious pattern indeed, but still intangible.

Their evidence was strong enough to raise questions but not fully exonerate her from official condemnation. Meanwhile, Baron Ulric's presence flitted in and out of the corridors all day, a looming shadow that stoked tension whenever he appeared with that cool, appraising stare.

An hour before the final meal, Cassandra retreated to her modest chamber, craving a moment's respite from the ceaseless distrust. The door closed behind her with a quiet click, shutting out the corridor. She set her belt pouch aside and ran a hand over her face, trying to dispel the throbbing headache building between her temples.

Her chamber was dim. A single candle on the rickety table offered meager light, flickering over the small basin of water. She dipped her hands in, relishing the coolness on her overheated skin. The memory of Taron's fervent promise stayed with her, mingled with the sting of Ulric's veiled threats at the council table. What a coil of stress and longing.

A soft rap sounded on the door. She stiffened. "Yes?"

"It's me," Taron said from the other side. The sound of his voice, hushed and near, sent her pulse jumping. She opened the door, glancing warily down the corridor, where no guard was immediately visible. Maybe they'd changed shifts. Taron slipped inside, tension visible in his posture.

He spoke before she could muster a greeting: "One of the knights found a witness, someone in the east corridor who might have seen a cloaked figure last night holding a strange wooden rod. Sir Barro is waiting for us in a side room near the kitchens to question the witness discreetly."

Her heart jolted. "Truly? Let's go, then."

He nodded, but lingered a beat. "We don't have to be in such a hurry, " He faltered, eyes traveling over her face.

"I came here to check on you. You haven't had a break all day."

Cassandra breathed in. Despite everything, a thread of warmth unspooled in her chest at the genuine concern in his expression. "I'll be fine," she said, gentler than she intended. "We need every clue we can get."

He lowered his voice further, standing so close the candlelight gilded half his face in gold. "Don't let my father's words get under your skin," he whispered

They were close enough that his breath ruffled a stray tendril of her hair. She could see the faint lines of strain around his eyes, the remnants of a man who'd endured too many nights of magical surges. And something else, a stirring spark, which she felt echo inside her. Heat coiled low in her belly, an unbidden response that tugged at the boundary between anger and desire. It was enough to make her heart skip.

"My father is not as powerful as he wants you to believe. The knights are starting to question his approach. If you remain steady, you'll find more allies."

"I, I'll remember," she managed, stepping past him, half afraid that if she let herself linger on the tension, she might do something reckless. She grabbed her belt pouch. "Shall we?"

A tight nod from him, almost reluctant. "Yes. Let's go."

THEY FOUND Sir Barro in a cramped side room off the kitchens, one typically used for storing sacks of flour. The

knight stood beside a slight figure, a young man in scuffed boots, wringing his cap in his hands. Cassandra guessed he was some sort of under-servant or runner. The air smelled faintly of yeast and spices from the kitchen next door. Taron gently closed the door behind them.

"Tell them what you told me," Barro instructed, voice gruff but not unkind. "Start from last night's second bell."

The servant swallowed, gaze darting between Taron and Cassandra. "I, I was finishing my chores, see," he began. "Was about to head upstairs to the scullery chamber when I heard footsteps. Odd, because it was late, most folks abed." He ran a thumb over his cap's frayed seam. "I look up and see a cloaked figure darting around the corner. Could barely catch a glimpse, but the shape was tall, maybe broad in the shoulders. Held sumthin'... like a carved staff or rod. But real short, more like a thick baton maybe. Then, out the window, I saw them vanish across the courtyard shadow, heading for the orchard path."

Cassandra's chest tightened. She folded her arms. "Did you see the face at all?"

He shook his head. "No, mistress. All I saw was a flicker of...some silver thread? Painted on the cloak? Coulda been a crest or some fancy design. I didn't get close." He looked down, clearly embarrassed at the admission of fear. "But the shape moved with purpose, that's for certain."

Taron exchanged a look with Cassandra. "This was after the second bell?" Taron asked. "Around midnight?"

"Just shy of it," the servant confirmed. "I only mention

it 'cause folks say you was forging ledgers or some nonsense at that very hour, mistress, but I saw you nowhere. Instead, that cloak... I don't know who it was, but it made me uneasy."

A swirl of relief and anger rose in Cassandra's chest. A potential piece of exoneration, though it was just one witness. But it also hammered home how meticulously these conspirators timed everything.

Sir Barro nodded and cleared his throat. "You'll speak with me again tomorrow, yes? Official-like? In case we need a sworn statement?" The young man nodded nervously. "Good. That will be all."

After the man left, Taron exhaled. "Someone moving from inside the keep to the orchard path right as the forged ledger claims Cassandra was signing out rods. That's not a coincidence. This is exactly the proof we need... though Father will demand more."

Cassandra let out a slow breath, heart thudding. "We have a glimmer of hope. If we can tie that baton, rod, staff, whatever it was, to the runic rods you found bungled in the storeroom logs, that might help."

Sir Barro's jaw set. "I'll do all in my power to verify it. But whoever this saboteur is, they're no mere petty thief. They know runes well, forging sign-outs, tampering with wards." He paused. "And they have some measure of authority or stealth, getting around the orchard watch."

The three of them stood there, the hush in the storeroom only broken by a distant clatter of pots from the kitchen. Cassandra's pulse still hammered from the possibility that this might be the break they needed, at least enough to keep Ulric from cracking down on her overnight. But she also felt the weight of the saboteur's cunning. If this figure had freedom to roam and vanish that easily, they might strike again soon.

"Thank you, Sir Barro," Cassandra murmured, letting genuine gratitude edge her voice. He gave a brusque nod, and she realized anew how precarious her position was: A single slip, and all these half-substantiated pieces could blow up in her face.

Taron gently guided her toward the door with a barely-there touch on her elbow. His eyes glimmered with an intensity she read as both protective resolve...and something more that made her stomach flutter. They stepped out into the corridor's dim light, leaving Barro behind.

"We'll keep going," Taron said quietly when they were alone. His words carried more weight than their brevity suggested. "For now, try to rest if you can tonight. If another surge hits me, I'll send for you."

She looked up at him, the corridor's sconce casting warm shadows across his angular features. The memory of his voice telling her that he wouldn't let them destroy her again flickered in her mind, stirring her heart. "I will," she whispered. "And you, keep your aura steady. Pull me from my bed if you must." The attempt at wry humor came out softer than she expected.

He smiled, pulse flickering at his throat. "Don't tempt me," he said, a hint of something close to longing glimmering in his eyes. "Sleep well, Cassandra."

Without another word, he turned and strode away

toward a side passage. She felt the space he left behind acutely, a tangible absence that made her realize just how aware she had become of his presence. Exhaling shakily, she wrapped her arms around herself and made her way back to the main corridor that led to her chamber. Though exhaustion weighed on her, she felt the spark of new determination.

They had uncovered more evidence today, a near certainty that there was indeed a hidden figure, forging signatures and slipping into the orchard at midnight. The sabotage was real, and it pointed away from her. All she had to do was keep following the trail, stave off malicious rumors, keep Taron from fracturing under pressure, and endure Ulric's manipulative scrutiny. Just the thought of it made her head throb.

But if she succeeded, maybe she could finally prove that witches did not deserve the keep's scorn. Maybe she could save Taron, and herself, from the shadows creeping in these halls. She pushed open her chamber door, stepping into the lonely dimness. Tomorrow promised fresh battles in the corridor of half-lies, but for tonight, she would cling to the spark of hope that not everyone in the barony believed her a traitor.

She could still feel the warmth of Taron's hand lightly brushing hers, the resolution in his voice when he insisted he would fight for her this time. That faint thrill interlaced with her fatigue as she slipped onto her narrow bed, letting the candlelight waver across the stone walls. Sleep was an elusive promise, but she closed her eyes on the thought that, for once, she might not be waging this battle alone.

At last, the hush of the keep enveloped her, though her mind remained crowded with the revelations of the day. The sabotage was deeper than she'd feared, the conspirator more cunning. She breathed slowly, counting each inhale until dreamless rest claimed her. Tomorrow, she vowed, they would press even harder to unmask the forger, even if Baron Ulric stood in their path, even if it meant braving a fresh onslaught of accusations. And if Taron's aura flared again before dawn, so be it. She would answer that call to keep him safe.

In the stillness, the single candle guttered, sending shadows flitting across her table. As Cassandra's thoughts finally began to still, she clung to one last sliver of comfort in this fortress of suspicion: despite the swirling illusions of conspiracy, she was not powerless. She had the truth, and a vow from the one man whose betrayal had once shattered her heart.

And between those fragile, uneasy alliances, she might yet find a way not just to survive this intrigue, but to truly change the kingdom's view of witches.

She fell asleep with her talisman clenched in her palm, warding against the darkness beyond her door.

Cassandra stood just beyond the courtyard's arched entry, half-hidden in the dusky shadows cast by the morning sun. The air carried crisp hints of hay and the earthy odor of horses, mingling with the whispered chatter of guards stationed along the walls. Her heart pounded a little quicker than she liked to admit; every sense told her something was off. For too many days, strange runic forgeries and rumored infiltrators had kept her constantly on edge, as if the very stones of Baron Ulric's keep might conspire against her.

Yet here she was, crouched near a row of barrel planters, scanning the courtyard for any sign of immediate threat. She would have given anything to retreat back to her forest enclave, to vanish among the pines that once sheltered her. But Taron was not safe, nor was the keep itself, and the knowledge bound her more tightly than any rope could.

A firm step sounded behind her, and she turned just

enough to see Sir Barro, stoic, broad-shouldered, and armed in the practical way that favored function over pomp. His interest lay not in her but in a horse-drawn wagon parked at the far edge of the courtyard. Dust clung to its wheels, as though it had come by long roads without official notice.

"There," Barro murmured. He tipped his chin in its direction. "That wagon showed up at dawn. Manifest claims it's delivering new warding staves." His tone told her he believed otherwise.

Cassandra's eyes drifted to the crates stacked on the wagon bed. Nothing outwardly unusual, a scattering of planks, ropes, and battered tarps, but the single emblem scrawled on one side made her stomach tighten. It was faint, only visible if someone knew exactly what to look for: a half-finished rune, incomplete but reminiscent of the sabotage markings they'd found carved into the farmland's warding posts. She suppressed a shiver.

"What did the driver tell you?" she asked, keeping her voice low.

Barro's expression never changed. "That he answered the keep's summons for new supplies. Supposedly we're short on everything, from feed to runic rods. But I compared his cargo slip to the official archives, none of it lines up."

Cassandra exhaled, tension bracing her shoulders. Another piece of the sabotage puzzle falling into place. First forged signatures in the storeroom ledgers, now a wagon carrying runic goods that no one had requested. "We have to be certain," she said quietly. "If we seize the wagon without proof, someone will twist it on me, accuse me of meddling or cooking up false claims."

Barro lifted one gauntleted hand. "Understood. But look closely at that crate." He guided her to a vantage behind a tall set of stacked hay bales. There, the symbol became clearer: angled lines forming a partial curve. "Matches the runes we found etched into the orchard posts."

Hearing that, Cassandra's chest knotted. She thought of the orchard wards nearly collapsing, Taron's aura spiking into a near-surge as a result. Another wave of anger rippled through her as she recalled the late nights spent investigating. "We can't let whoever is behind this slip away again," she said. "If those runes are inside the wagon or embedded on the rods, they could destabilize Taron all over the barony."

As if conjured by her words, Taron emerged from a corridor leading to the lesser stables, face drawn and pale. The bruised shadows under his hazel eyes broadcast his exhaustion. She hadn't seen him since dawn, but she could guess he'd spent the early hours wrestling with the remnants of last night's magical flare, one that had charred fresh scorch marks onto the walls of his chamber. He walked carefully, leaning more on his left foot as if it grounded him. In the swirling undercurrent of watchful stares, Cassandra spotted how the common folk in the courtyard noticed him. Knights paused in mid-step. Two passing servants quickly dipped their heads. She glimpsed a mixture of awe and apprehension in their expressions: some feared the raw power Taron could unleash if his aura slipped again, others recognized how determined he was to protect them, despite his father's cold maneuvers.

Her heart twisted. Only a few weeks ago, seeing Taron appear in the courtyard might have brought out her anger over his past betrayal, letting her be exiled while staying silent. Now, conflicting emotions tangled in her chest: wariness, yes, but also empathy for the constant burden he carried. She sensed his magical aura fluttering against her own awareness, as if it recognized her presence.

"Cassandra," he said softly once within earshot, voice still edged with fatigue. He offered Barro a polite nod, then looked between them. "I saw the wagon." His gaze flicked to the emblem half-hidden by the tarp. "What have you learned?"

She filled him in on their suspicions, how the crates might be loaded with sabotage runes, that the cargo slip was forged. Taron's mouth flattened in a grim line, and a tiny spark crackled around the cuff on his wrist. She placed a gentle hand on his forearm at once, offering a subtle grounding push of magic. His breath shuddered but steadied.

"Easy," Cassandra murmured. He nodded, his shoulders easing under her touch.

"I can't afford another surge, not here," Taron said. "If those runic rods are tampered with, they could link to my aura the moment they're brought into the keep." He pressed the heel of his hand to his brow. "I'm...still recovering from last night. Your potions help, but the effect is short-lived."

Barro glanced around, scanning for eavesdroppers.

"We can't just seize the crates in broad daylight," he muttered. "Half the keep might see it as another reason to pin blame on Mistress Cassandra."

Cassandra couldn't deny the tightness that statement inflicted. Even after she'd healed an injured guard or two, a portion of the barony's population still viewed her as the prime suspect for sabotage. If the saboteurs had come up with another cunning trap, she had to be more discreet than ever. She already felt the eyes of a few passing stewards and lesser-ranking knights. Any show of aggression on her part might feed the rumor flames.

Footsteps rustled behind them, two guards in battered armor, each wearing the crest of House Ulric pinned to their shoulders. They hovered uncertainly, flicking cautious glances Taron's way. One, a younger knight with sandy hair, cleared his throat.

"My lord," the younger knight said. "There have been… reports. Cloaked figures near the gates at dawn. They wore gray, maybe black, no crest. Slipped away before we could see their faces."

Cassandra's pulse kicked. Cloaked strangers lurking just beyond the keep. Another jigsaw piece. She caught Taron's eye, and saw the worry brimming there. Part of her was fiercely relieved to see confirmation that she wasn't the only one who'd glimpsed these silhouettes in the dark corridors or orchard paths. Saboteurs had to be coordinating these deliveries, using bribes, forging documents, and planting illusions.

"Which gate?" Taron asked, tone sharpened by tension.

"The eastern postern," the knight replied. "They stood there no more than a minute, then vanished. We're short-staffed, so I couldn't pursue without leaving the gate unguarded."

Taron nodded. "Thank you for alerting us. Keep a watchful eye. And if you see them again..."

"Yes, my lord," the knight said, his companion echoing a salute before they walked off toward the open yard.

Cassandra let out a slow, measured breath, trying to slot this new piece into the puzzle. "The eastern postern is near the orchard path, not far from where wards were tampered with before," she pointed out.

Sir Barro's face was grim. "We should search that wagon soon. If it's loaded with runes meant to spark Taron's power, we can't allow them to be distributed. But you're right, too public a confrontation puts Cassandra at risk. We need tact."

A flicker of movement drew Cassandra's attention. In the courtyard's center, a half-dozen knights had gathered. Some wore open curiosity, others carried the guarded stance of men uncertain whether to trust the figure wearing the runic cuff. Cassandra recognized a few of them, including a tall, broad-chested man named Holt, one of the older knights who had grown silent whenever she passed.

Another was a younger knight with a scar across his nose, who frowned at her whenever the word "witch" was muttered in the corridors. She'd never learned his name, only endured his suspicious glances. Yet there they stood, not fleeing from Taron or from her.

Taron drew a breath and stepped forward, shoulders squared, though the tremor in his hands betrayed his lingering exhaustion. Cassandra moved discreetly closer in case his magic spiked again.

"We're investigating suspicious cargo," Taron called out, raising his voice so the knights could hear. "Baron Ulric's keep is thick with rumors of infiltration, and we will not ignore them. My father may be devoted to official procedures, but time is short, who among you is ready to help discover the truth?"

An murmur rippled through the group. At the edges of the courtyard, a few villagers hovered, arms burdened with baskets or crates, obviously torn between curiosity and fear. Cassandra flexed her fingers, recalling how often she'd been glared at. This was the same keep that once exiled her without a second thought. Today, it seemed on the verge of acknowledging that perhaps she wasn't the root of all evil. The irony tasted bitter.

For an instant, no one spoke. Then Holt, the older knight, cleared his throat. "My lord, I admit I initially doubted Mistress Cassandra's intentions." His deep voice carried, echoing under the pale morning sky. "But I've seen signs: footprints matching no one here, runic chalk found in places she never visited. I can't stand by while you face sabotage alone. Count me in."

CHAPTER
SIX

A rush of relief traveled through Cassandra's veins. She nodded at Holt, her chest lightening fractionally. Another knight, one with a thick braid of chestnut hair, stepped forward to add, "We've all heard the talk: illusions of sabotage pinned on her. But it's grown too neat, too consistent. I fear we've been fooled by a puppet master behind the scenes."

A third knight, arms folded over a battered cuirass, exhaled. "My family lives in the farmland. Heard from a cousin that a figure in a dark cloak was spotted tampering with a warding post a fortnight back... We need to uproot this threat before it grows worse."

In that moment, while faces turned warily or hopefully toward Taron and Cassandra, she felt an odd pang inside her chest. After weeks of standing alone, battered by allegations, she was seeing a shift. Not a sweeping absolution, but a handful of knights who recognized she might be the only one capable of protecting Taron, and by extension, all of them. The tension in her shoulders loosened by a hair.

Taron's posture straightened, some color returning to his face. "Then help us," he said simply. "We suspect the wagon in the far corner there." He pointed to where the driver stood, arms folded, looking bored or perhaps impatient. "We plan to search it. Properly. If the cargo is innocuous, so be it. But if we find sabotage runes…"

He trailed off, letting the implication hang. Cassandra watched hesitation flit across the gathered men's features. With Baron Ulric absent, for the moment, some knights might worry about overstepping authority. But Taron was the baron's son, and given the barony's current anxieties, no one seemed eager to stand in his way.

Barro spoke up, voice gruff. "We'll need witnesses if we open those crates, or the saboteur might claim we tampered ourselves. Holt, you'll come with us?"

Holt nodded. "Aye."

Cassandra gathered her courage. "We'll be careful. But if you see anything with a half-finished rune, report it immediately. Don't let it be carried deeper into the keep, or Taron's aura might get drawn into another surge."

She belatedly realized how much authority laced her voice. Weeks ago, no one would have listened to her. Now, Holt and the other knights gave short nods of respect. She swallowed, unsure whether to feel anxious or motivated.

"Driver's still waiting," Taron murmured. "Let's move before he decides to disappear."

They crossed the courtyard as a small unit. Cassandra, Taron, Barro, Holt, and two younger knights trailing at a distance. Several villagers parted to let them pass, murmuring and exchanging glances. She overheard one woman whisper, "That's Baron Ulric's son, poor lad," and another hiss back, "Don't pity him too soon, he's got that witch at his side." The words stung, but she pressed forward, telling herself that forging alliances with a few was better than being beloved by none.

The wagon driver, a lanky fellow wearing a threadbare cloak, noticed them. He gave a half-smile, though his grip on the reins tensed. "Mornin', my lord. Here to inspect the goods you requested?" His gaze flicked warily over Cassandra.

Taron's eyes narrowed. "There's been some confusion about the request. We'd like to confirm your paperwork."

"Paperwork, right." The driver patted a small pouch at his belt, pulling out a parchment. His hand shook slightly, noticeable enough that Cassandra felt her pulse tick higher. He offered it to Sir Barro, who accepted it with practiced calm.

Barro scanned the parchment, brow creasing. "This seal is...an older version of the barony's crest, seldom used." He glanced at the driver. "Where'd you obtain it?"

"From...your man at the gates, passed it along with the message," the driver said quickly, too quickly. He averted his eyes. "Said the barony needed these staves and rods for urgent farmland repairs."

Holt glanced at the parchment over Barro's shoulder, his expression darkening. "This is definitely forged. Our crest changed some details months ago. Yours references the older stylized falcon, not the new variant."

The driver gave a shrug, the gesture evidently meant to seem casual. Sweat beaded on his temple. "I, I'm just the messenger, sirs. If that's an old crest, maybe it was an older slip. Could've been lying around. Who's to say?"

Taron's voice rumbled quietly. "We'll check the crates regardless."

Cassandra moved to the wagon's side, noticing now that the driver slid half a step to intercept her. "Mind yourself," he said. "If you're not the steward or the baron, you've got no right rummaging through my goods."

She lifted her chin. "I'm acting on behalf of Lord Taron. If you have nothing to hide, let us see."

His eyes darted to Taron, then to the group of knights. Realizing he had no advantage, the man muttered something under his breath and stepped aside. Cassandra braced herself on the wagon's wooden slats and surveyed the crates. With Holt and Barro's help, she loosened the rope that held one box shut. The driver paced behind them, arms twitchy, as if weighing whether to bolt.

Cassandra pried the lid open. Inside lay a row of short rods, each carved from some pale wood. Warding rods or so it seemed. The surface was etched with runic lines, but even in the early sunlight, she spotted smears of fresh ink and faintly scratched scribbles, distinct from traditional wards. She inhaled, letting her senses extend. A prickle of energy made her hand recoil, as though the rods carried a twisting heat she recognized from sabotage attempts.

"These runes are incomplete," she muttered. "And they're shaping the form of a siphon, if Taron's aura interacts with them, it could create feedback." She shot Taron a warning look over her shoulder.

He stepped closer, looked down at them, a flicker dancing across his own cuff runes. "It's the same sabotage pattern we saw near the orchard." His voice turned grim. "Intended to disrupt the established wards and intensify my surges."

Holt gave Barro a significant nod. "This confirms it. No honest supplies would be scrawled with these partial runes."

Barro faced the driver. "You said you were told to bring these here. Who gave the order?"

The man licked his lips. "I...not sure. A figure in a cloak approached me in the night, said he was from the keep, asked me to deliver these rods. Promised good coin." He spread his hands, desperation creeping into his tone. "I didn't ask names. Just trying to feed my family."

Cassandra believed he might be a pawn more than a mastermind. "Did he have a crest or any distinguishing symbol?"

The driver hesitated, then blinked. "He wore gloves, I remember that. I saw a glint of something silver embroidered on his cloak. Not the baron's falcon, though. Something else." He squirmed under their scrutiny. "Look, that's all I know."

Taron nodded, though his face remained etched with tension. "Take the rods into custody. Holt, Barro, secure them someplace no one else can tamper with them. Then we'll speak with the gatehouse guards who might've seen this cloaked figure. We cannot let these rods vanish."

Barro made a hand sign to a couple of listening knights, who stepped forward to gather the crates. Everyone moved carefully with the rods, wary not to trigger any reactive magic. Taron's presence alone was risky. Cassandra quietly suppressed a surge of dread: if these rods were set up in farmland or placed near Taron's chamber, the damage might be catastrophic. She recalled the farmland's near-ruinous sabotage and how it had almost broken Taron's control. This had to stop.

Meanwhile, the driver sagged against the wagon's side, relief flickering across his face once no one arrested him outright. "I swear, I didn't know they were harmful. I was just delivering them." He swallowed. "Am…am I free to go?"

Taron considered him. "You'll wait here until we've confirmed some details. I won't have you vanish the moment we turn our backs."

The man nodded miserably, dropping to sit on the wagon's edge. Cassandra felt a pang of guarded sympathy. He likely wasn't the hidden architect of these schemes, only another tool.

Sir Barro handed the forged documents to one of the other knights. "Take these to the scribe for verification. Make an official note that the seal is outdated. Then see that the rods are locked in the storerooms under guard, you two," he said, pointing to the younger knights, "escort the driver for questioning."

With that, a swirl of purposeful activity swept across the courtyard. A handful of onlookers parted like startled birds, eyes wide at the uncovered sabotage. Whispers rose among them, carrying words like "Illicit runes" and "Taron's power." Cassandra tried not to flinch at the conspiracy-laden stares but couldn't ignore the tight coil of anxiety in her belly.

Taron touched her shoulder briefly, drawing her attention. "Thank you for noticing the runes," he said softly. "You've likely saved us from a new wave of sabotage."

She swallowed. "We still need more answers. Cloaked figures at dawn…someone forging official documents… There's a network at play." In the shifting sunlight, she noticed worry etched deeper in Taron's brow, a subtle tremor in his wrist cuff. She pressed her palm to his forearm again, channeling a sliver of calm. "Are you all right?"

He let out a shaky breath. "I'm…managing. The potion you gave me helps, but my magic's never truly at rest. Watching you handle those rods, I felt it stir, like it recognized the sabotage." He lowered his voice. "I can't keep relying on quick fixes."

"If the potion's not enough, we'll find another way. You've been carrying this for so long—longer than you should have to." Her tone softened, a gentle plea hidden in her words. "Let me help you before it gets worse."

He hesitated, his gaze flickering to the floor before meeting hers again. "It's not just about the magic. It's me.

Every time it stirs, it reminds me of what I am, what I've done. No potion can fix that."

Her hand hovered near his, then rested lightly on his forearm, offering comfort without pressing too far. "Then let's focus on what we *can* do."

His lips twitched, almost forming a smile, but the weight in his eyes remained. "You don't know what it's like to feel like you'll lose control of everything you are."

Cassandra's heart twisted. She knew Taron's control hung by a thread. She also half-dreaded the day he might push his father aside and stand fully on his own. Not because she didn't want him to be free, but because that confrontation with Baron Ulric would be monumental, and possibly savage.

"Let's find out who orchestrates these shipments," she said. "We have enough knights on our side to do it quietly and efficiently."

He nodded. For a moment, their gazes locked, unspoken tension thrumming between them. She remembered the swirl of complicated feelings from the previous nights: regret, longing, the memory of his confession that he'd kept silent years ago only to save her from execution. Even now, a part of her still stung with that old betrayal. Another part, though, recognized how unfailingly he'd tried to protect her since she returned. They stood side by side, carrying the same burden but from different angles.

A frown curved across Taron's mouth. "Father's going to demand an update."

Cassandra stiffened. "Do we involve him directly now?

He's the baron, but… " she let her voice trail off, not wanting to push Taron too hard.

Taron's expression set. "In name, yes. But he might dismiss this discovery, belittle it as a ploy. He's refused to back me on investigating sabotage before." A flicker of anger flashed in his eyes. "I'm done waiting for his permission. If he wants to question me afterward, so be it."

A quiet jolt of satisfaction stirred in her chest, hearing him speak so decisively. "Then we do what needs to be done," she said simply. "And gather the proof to expose whoever is behind this."

They turned to rejoin the knights. Holt and Barro had organized a cluster near the keep's outer ramp, quietly discussing the next steps. Another pair of knights had guided the driver away, presumably to a side guardroom for further questioning. A wave of watchers lingered on the fringes, servants, minor stewards, a handful of villagers who'd delivered produce to the keep. Their wide eyes followed Cassandra, but no one dared approach. She could practically feel the tension in the air, as if everyone sensed the barony teetering on the brink of something big.

Holt beckoned them closer. "We plan to station two men at the storerooms while we examine those rods more thoroughly. If the saboteur tries to retrieve them, we'll have an ambush prepared. Meanwhile, I'll speak to the gatehouse stewards, see who was on duty when the driver arrived."

Sir Barro gave Taron a respectful dip of his head. "It might help if you or Mistress Cassandra also speak to any guard who glimpsed the cloaked visitors at dawn. We need to confirm if the sabotage and these deliveries are linked to the same group."

"I'll do it," Cassandra said. The swirl of determination in her chest overrode her usual caution. "They might be more willing to talk if Taron's presence isn't overshadowing them. No offense," she added, glancing at Taron.

He managed a tired half-smile. "None taken. Some guards do freeze up around my surges. Your approach could be less intimidating."

"Less intimidating for them, maybe," Holt muttered wryly, "but I imagine the saboteurs are plenty intimidated by you, Mistress Cassandra."

An odd hush followed those words. She couldn't tell if he meant it as a compliment or a remark on her rumored capacity for dangerous witchcraft. Still, she accepted the statement with a nod. "Where can I find them?"

Sir Barro gestured toward the keep's eastern wall. "They might be patrolling near the orchard side. A guard named Straithe. He reported seeing a glimpse of a figure just outside the gates. Let's check."

They split up. Taron stayed with Holt to confirm the wagon's inventory and quell the rising murmur among the keep's staff, while Cassandra accompanied Barro to the gatehouse path. A few knights peeled off to guard the storerooms. The courtyard's noise ebbed as she and Barro wove their way past the stable yard. Overhead, gulls circled, drawn inland from distant waterways, their plaintive cries underscoring the hush of tension below.

Trailing behind Barro's heavy stride, Cassandra

wondered if a handful of newly supportive knights would be enough to stifle a full-scale plot, one that might involve an entire ring of contacts, from bribed gate guards to well-placed saboteurs forging official documents. Yet, as she inhaled the morning air, she felt a flicker of hope. At least she wasn't alone now. Taron's stand had inspired a few to join them, men like Sir Barro who once eyed her with suspicion.

She brushed her palm over the small talisman at her neck, the one Miriana had gifted her. A quiet reassurance that her witchcraft was for healing, for protection, not for destruction. If sabotage threatened Taron's life, she would fight with all the magic and cunning she possessed.

When they reached the orchard side of the keep, the noise of daily chores faded. The orchard's neat rows of fruit trees started near the curtain wall, mingling with the faint scent of blossoms. A set of broad steps led to a side gate seldom used by official processions but favored by local workers heading to the farmland. Two guards loitered near a pair of large wooden doors set into the stone wall. One was a woman with braided hair pinned under a dented helm, and the other was a rangy man with a pockmarked cheek. They stood straighter as Barro approached.

"We're looking for Straithe," Barro said, voice low but firm.

"That would be me," said the man, inclining his head. "What's this about?"

Cassandra stepped forward, clearing her throat. "We've learned you saw a cloaked figure this morning, near dawn, lurking by the gate. We need every detail you can give."

Straithe's gaze flicked to Barro, then back to her. His shoulders twitched, uncertain. "I...yes, I glimpsed someone. Tall, wore a dark mantle with perhaps silver thread? Could've been a crest, but the light was poor. They hovered a moment, then the next thing I knew, they vanished around the orchard corner. By the time I unbolted the gate to follow, I found no trace."

She exchanged a quick glance with Barro. The mention of silver thread matched the driver's claim of seeing something silver on a cloak. "Anything else?" she pressed. "Did you hear them speak, catch any accent?"

"Nothing. It was quiet. They moved fast, almost like they knew the gate's patrol schedule." His mouth tightened. "And me, I only had the one lady guard here," he nodded toward his companion, "so we couldn't leave the gate unguarded for too long."

The woman, slightly shorter, wearing a worn surcoat, spoke up. "It's not the first time we've spotted someone skulking around. Last week, there was a rumor of footprints in the orchard after midnight, but no one saw who left them."

A flicker of exasperation roused in Cassandra. "We suspect these watchers are linked to the sabotage. They seem to come and go without detection. Possibly bribing or forging documents. Keep your eyes open. If you see them again, do not engage alone. Summon more knights."

Straithe nodded, though a line of skepticism marred

his forehead. "Understood. But I can't say we'll catch them in time. They slip away like shadows."

Barro grunted. "We'll set additional watch, especially around dawn. Thank you, both. Any new sightings, report to me or Sir Holt."

With that, they left the orchard gate behind. Cassandra's mind churned, trying to piece together the pattern: dark-cloaked watchers at dawn, attempted deliveries of sabotage rods, everything timed to keep the keep in a cycle of panic and confusion. If Taron's father refused to see the truth, the saboteurs might continue operating with impunity. She wrestled down a surge of frustration.

EIGHT

On their way back, they passed a cluster of orchard workers who paused, nodding respectfully to Barro but eyeing Cassandra with caution. For a fleeting moment, she glimpsed the life she might have lived if the barony had accepted her as a ward-crafter, walking these orchard rows, using her magic openly to bolster the fruit trees, tending to the land with a sense of purpose. She could almost see herself there, her hands alight with soft golden sigils, her heart lighter, her future clear.

But that dream had shattered the moment Taron began to change. At first, it had been subtle—the hesitant way he spoke to her when others were around, the way his gaze would dart to the horizon as if measuring what might happen if he let his affection show. The orchard had been their haven once, a place where they'd laughed, plotted wild futures, and stolen kisses under the sun-dappled boughs. But then came the day when his tone cooled, when he started speaking to her as if she were just another piece on the board of his father's ever-tightening game.

That was when she'd first realized Taron would succumb to his father's pressure, that the boy who had once loved her so fiercely would one day become a man bound to duty, not to her. She'd tried to reach him, but his father's shadow loomed too large. It hadn't taken long before his distance turned to silence, leaving her to wrestle with the betrayal on her own.

The orchard workers moved on, their murmurs lost in the breeze, and Cassandra forced herself back to the present. Those memories were a distraction, a reminder of a life that no longer existed. Now, the stakes were different —bigger than her broken heart or Taron's choices. If she didn't act, the saboteurs would rip the barony apart while the people here, from the workers to Barro himself, paid the price.

She let out a slow breath and quickened her pace, leaving the orchard and its ghosts behind.

Barro glanced her way. "Your presence rattles them, you know," he said quietly.

She sighed. "I'm well aware."

"But some of them are starting to see beyond the rumors. They watch you, yes, but they also see how Taron relies on your wards. You might earn their trust sooner than you think."

The unexpected encouragement caught her off guard. She offered him a short nod, a small gratitude flickering behind her eyes. "I hope so."

They circled back to the courtyard, where the wagon

still stood, now guarded by two of Holt's men. The crates had been moved, presumably locked away. The driver was nowhere in sight. But Taron was there, conferring with Holt in hushed tones. As soon as Cassandra approached, Taron's gaze shifted to her, relief slipping through his tired features.

"What did Straithe say?" he asked, voice subdued.

She relayed the information. Taron's lips tightened. "Matches the driver's mention of silver thread. So, it's likely one or two people orchestrating this from the shadows, paying couriers to deliver sabotage runes." He rubbed his temple. "We keep confirming there's a hidden adversary pulling these strings. But not who."

Holt nodded. "For now, we'll keep the rods under guard. Barro and I will draft an official record of the forgery. Then we must widen the orchard patrol...even if we're short-handed." He eyed Taron. "My lord, you'd best check in with the council soon. They'll be clamoring for an explanation if they see these crates seized."

Taron huffed a grim laugh. "So be it. Cassandra, you,"

"I'll go with you," she said, a bit stiffer than intended. "I doubt the council will be gentle about this. Someone's bound to smear me with yet more accusations." She forced calm into her tone. "Unless you want me searching for more leads elsewhere...?"

He hesitated, as though torn between wanting to shield her from the council's hostility and needing her at his side. "I'd rather have you there," he admitted quietly. "You can confirm the malicious runes. And if father tries to cast blame, well, your expertise on warding sabotage is crucial."

She nodded, ignoring the swirl in her stomach. She loathed the keep's councils: gatherings full of suspicious murmurs, nobles who resented her presence as an exiled witch forcibly brought back. But Taron was right. If she didn't speak up herself, the sabotage might be spun in all manner of ways, and rumors linking her to forged rods would flourish unchecked.

Sir Barro dipped his head. "I'll handle the official inventory of the crates. If anything arises, I'll notify you both at once."

Cassandra and Taron left the courtyard, stepping through a smaller door leading into the keep's interior corridors. The hush of stone hallways enveloped them, muffling the outdoor clamor. A single guard offered them a crisp salute, and Taron acknowledged it absently. Between them, the weight of unspoken thoughts pressed heavily.

Finally, Cassandra broke the silence. "Are you braced for your father's response? You know he'll try to twist this."

Taron sighed, running a hand through his hair. "I'm prepared to stand my ground. I may not have official baronial status yet, but I won't let him ignore the threat these rods pose. Not after we nearly lost farmland to sabotage last time."

She studied his profile, the slight tautness around his mouth. "If it gets heated..."

"I'll handle him," Taron said. Then, quieter, "Thank

you for not stepping away. I know dealing with the council can't be easy for you."

She swallowed. "Hardly. But this affects everyone. And you," She hesitated, letting a flicker of vulnerability surface. "I won't watch them sabotage your magic again, Taron."

He slowed, eyes flicking to her face. Something in his expression softened. "Cassandra..."

He stopped walking altogether, turning to face her fully. His voice was low but steady, threaded with concern. "You've been carrying something since we left the orchard, haven't you? It's not just the sabotage or the council. It's...what happened back then. The way I handled things. The way I handled *us*."

Her throat tightened, and she looked away, her gaze skimming over the stone walls as though the answers lay hidden in the cracks. "It's nothing we can change now. I know the pressures you were under—your father's expectations, the barony's demands. I don't hold it against you."

"But it weighs on you," he pressed gently, stepping closer. "I saw it in your eyes earlier, when we passed the orchard workers. That life we talked about, the one we dreamed of, it wasn't just a fantasy for you. It was real. And I let my father's ambitions take it away from you. From *us*."

She shook her head, but he caught her hand, his touch firm yet tender. "You've changed, Taron. I know that. You're not the same man who stood silent when his father pushed me out."

"Maybe," he admitted, his thumb brushing over her

knuckles. "But I've done nothing to prove to you that I'll never let it happen again. Not yet." He searched her face, his voice rough with emotion. "Cassandra, I'm stronger now. I've learned to stand on my own, to push back against his control. I'm not the boy who faltered when it mattered most. I *will* prove it to you. I'll earn back your full trust. I'll show you how much you mean to me; how much you've *always* meant."

Her lips parted, and for a moment, she couldn't find words. His sincerity was so raw, so unguarded, that it left her breathless. "Taron," she began, but he shook his head slightly, a faint smile tugging at his lips.

"Don't tell me you already know," he murmured. "Let me show you. Let me make it undeniable."

The intensity of his gaze held hers captive, and before she could respond, he leaned in, his hand coming up to cradle her cheek. His lips brushed hers, tentative at first, as though seeking permission. When she didn't pull away— when she leaned into him, her fingers curling into the fabric of his tunic deepened the kiss, pouring all his unspoken promises into it.

Her other hand slid to his chest, feeling the steady thrum of his heartbeat beneath her palm. The world around them seemed to fade—the cold stone walls, the weight of sabotage, the looming council. All that remained was the warmth of his lips, the familiar scent of him, the way his hand at her waist held her like he couldn't bear to let go.

When they finally broke apart, her breath came

uneven, her forehead resting lightly against his. "You don't have to prove anything, Taron. You already have."

But he shook his head again, his voice steady despite the emotion lacing it. "Not enough. Not yet. But I will. Every day, for as long as you'll have me."

She met his gaze, her heart caught between the ache of old wounds and the promise of something new. And when he kissed her again, she let herself believe, just for a moment, that they might finally be free of the past.

Footsteps echoed from behind, a trio of servants passing through with a stack of linens. The moment was snuffed out before he could finish. She saw regret behind his gaze, and then he resumed walking. Perhaps it was better that way; neither of them had time to dwell on half-formed confessions. Too many dangers prowled the keep's corners.

They would present the evidence soon, no doubt receiving a frosty reception from Baron Ulric and whatever coterie of counselors he'd assembled this morning. Yet Cassandra clung to a spark of determination. For the first time, a handful of knights had stepped forward to support them. She'd just uncovered solid, tangible sabotage rods. She was no longer alone, no longer the exiled witch cowering in the keep's shadows. The saboteur's circle might still outnumber them, but the tide felt like it was turning. If she and Taron could keep forging alliances, exposing each link in the saboteur's chain, they just might root out this threat before it plunged Taron or the barony into chaos.

They reached the corridor leading to the council

chamber. Its arched doorway stood at the far end, devoid of the usual cluster of courtiers, likely because the meeting time had not yet been set. Taron paused, turning to face her. In the lantern-lit hush, his gaze flicked over her features as if memorizing them. A flush of warmth spiraled through her chest, an unspoken reminder of the closeness that once existed between them, the possibility that still lingered behind their anger and guilt.

He opened his mouth to speak, but the faint thunder of approaching footsteps made them both tense. A steward in elaborate but slightly frayed attire rounded the corner, halting with mild surprise at seeing them.

"My lord, Mistress Cassandra," the steward greeted, dipping his head. "The baron convenes a council soon. He demands your presence."

Taron glanced at Cassandra. "We expected as much. Let's not keep him waiting." His eyes flicked back to the steward. "First, gather any knights who can confirm our findings about the sabotaged supplies."

The steward paled a fraction, nodded, and rushed off.

Cassandra let out a measured breath. Together, side by side, she and Taron headed down the corridor to face whatever waited behind those imposing double doors. She tried to quell the dread that coiled in her stomach. The memory of that wagon's runic crates, the driver's anxious face, the cloak rumored to bear silver thread, these images wheeled through her mind in a swirl of questions.

Every step reminded her of the precarious balance they were on old resentments, new conspiracies, a father who'd once threatened her life, and the barony's next surge of panic looming just out of sight. Yet for all that, she felt a flicker of steady resolve. She had allies now, a handful of knights, a few open-minded guards, and Taron himself, battered by guilt but resolute in forging a different path.

At the threshold of the council chamber, they paused. Taron's breathing sounded tight, but he offered her a faint, fleeting smile of encouragement. His presence lent her strength, and the tension that had once roiled between them, born of betrayal, now simmered into a fierce, shared determination. She pressed her hand lightly against her belt pouch, where warding chalk and a dose of potion remained. One final breath, and she readied herself.

They stepped inside, prepared to present the evidence of sabotage rods and infiltration to any who would listen, and equally ready to battle the baron's dismissive glare if he tried to quash them. Because the keep's future, and Taron's life, depended on unmasking the saboteur before fear locked every door.

As the chamber doors closed, Cassandra felt that tremor of unease tighten in her belly. But she also felt a spark of hope that had long eluded her. A handful of knights had believed her enough to join this cause. There were watchers in cloaks lurking outside, yes, but they were not unstoppable. The new runic rods, disproven and confiscated, had revealed a crucial key to the conspirators' methods.

She squared her shoulders. Allies stood at the gates. Not enough to guarantee victory, but enough to give their fight purpose. With Taron at her side, she was determined to chase down every shadow until she exposed the heart of the conspiracy. Because in this precarious fortress of secrets, she had found something she'd barely dared to hope for again: people willing to trust her, and perhaps, in time, trust witches at large.

No matter what Baron Ulric or the rival saboteur had in store, Cassandra refused to back down. She would root out the threat, protect Taron, and gods willing, carve a path toward a future where witches and nobles no longer had to clash. Even if it meant standing before a council that despised her, even if it meant braving sabotage at every turn, she would not break.

And as they stepped forward into the council chamber, the memory of that timid driver, the suspicious rods, and the faint silver threads swirled through her mind like a warning. Shrouded enemies still lurked, but so did new allies, she just had to ensure those allies multiplied before darkness swallowed them whole.

NINE

Cassandra's pulse thundered in her ears as she entered the council chamber, every footstep echoing on the polished stones. The tall double doors groaned behind her, shutting out what little natural light flooded the corridor. Within, gloom gathered in the high-raftered ceiling, broken only by the flicker of wall-mounted lanterns. It reminded her of a looming judgment hall rather than a place of measured governance.

She had been summoned by Baron Ulric the moment the midday bell tolled, no explanation, no time to catch her breath, only an abrupt courier bursting into her cramped sleeping chamber with a clipped demand for her immediate presence. All morning, eddies of tension had hung in the keep, subtle but unmistakable in the stiffness of passing knights and the nervous glances of servants.

Forcing a steady breath, she advanced into the room. More than a dozen faces turned her way. Some belonged to the barony's minor nobles, others to stewards and lesser advisors who assisted in daily administration. She sensed their discomfort, tinged with open curiosity. A hush fell at her arrival, broken only by the scratch of a scribe's quill on parchment.

She fought the urge to smooth the loose braid that draped over her shoulder, its strands a deep, auburn brown, glinting faintly in the flickering lanterns. Her skin, sun-warmed and freckled from long hours outdoors crafting wards, seemed to set her apart from the pale refinement of the nobles, many of whom avoided the fields altogether.

She straightened her spine, conscious of her stature—not tall, but lean and wiry from years of physical work. Her sharp, storm-gray eyes swept across the room, holding each gaze for just long enough to project confidence, even as unease curled at the edges of her mind.

She knew she cut an unconventional figure in this chamber, a world away from the courtly elegance the nobles were accustomed to. Her plain, practical tunic and leather boots, though clean, bore the subtle wear of her trade, a stark contrast to the silks and embroidery surrounding her. But even as she felt the weight of their stares, she refused to shrink under their scrutiny. She had earned her place here through skill, not privilege, and she would not let herself falter now.

Baron Ulric occupied his usual seat at the head of the long wooden table, though calling it a seat seemed too modest. Even without a regal throne, he presided over the gathering as if the entire keep were an extension of himself. His broad shoulders filled out a dark doublet adorned with understated flourishes of silver thread forming the baronial crest. Candlelight highlighted the steel-gray in his hair, and lines of displeasure formed at the corners of his mouth.

"Mistress Cassandra." His voice cut the hush like a blade. He did not stand, nor did he give her the courtesy of gentler tones. He gestured for her to take a position at a smaller bench along the side. "I trust you've realized the urgency of this meeting."

She refused to curtsy, though her palms had begun to sweat. Her eyes flicked over the other attendees: a handful of councilors she recognized from prior gatherings, some with suspicion etched in their stares. Among them, she recognized a steward who had dogged her suspiciously before, a pair of knights pinned to the wall like watchful hawks, and Sir Barro, standing near the far side with folded arms. The will to bristle rose in her chest, but she kept her posture unwavering and her chin level.

"You summoned me, my lord," she said, her voice calm but firm. "I'm here."

Ulric's jaw tightened, faintly revealing his displeasure at her directness. "We've had reports," he began, "that Taron's magic is again in flux. Indeed, new disturbances in the farmland wards suggest that he's edging toward another surge. And yet, you", his eyes flicked over her in a gesture that felt more like condemnation than simple scrutiny, "appear to be making no progress in stabilizing him."

A muscle tightened in Cassandra's back. Memories of

Taron's last near-disastrous surge still haunted her; she had knelt in his chamber, forcing what little healing magic she could muster into him. She could recall the flicker of his eyes, the strangled breath as their wards collided to contain his outpouring of energy. If not for her, he might have razed a corridor or worse. Yet at every turn since, it felt as though Ulric or one of his allies found a way to twist Taron's pace of recovery into a failing on Cassandra's part.

She inhaled slowly. "Taron's condition can't be resolved overnight, my lord. You know the sabotage has worsened the wards. If we don't address whoever is tampering with them, there's no anchor capable of containing him fully."

There was a faint rustle from one of the seated lords, a form of dissatisfaction or boredom. Ulric latched onto her words. "Sabotage," he repeated with a dismissive snort. "An excuse you've brandished since the day you set foot in this keep. I tire of hearing it, footprints in the orchard, runic rods you claim you never signed out, and all the rest. If you had real proof, you'd have offered it by now."

She felt her anger kindle, a low burn starting in her chest. She thought of the suspicious crates that had turned up in the courtyard, etched with cryptic runes meant to disrupt Taron's wards. She thought of the forged ledgers implicating her. Some of that evidence was partial, enough to stoke doubt among a handful of knights, but apparently not enough to sway the baron's official stance. He would not even grant the courtesy of an open investigation.

Cassandra's mouth felt bone-dry. "My lord," she managed, "the attempts to frame me are too consistent and too methodical to be mere rumor. Even Sir Barro has seen the,"

Ulric's palm slammed onto the table, and the scribe at its far edge jumped in alarm. "You speak as though you command my knights and my resources. You do not," he said, voice cutting. "I stand witness each day to Taron's struggle. If your wards were effective, he would not be stumbling through the keep at all hours, hardly able to contain what leaks from his aura. If you were truly the cunning ward-crafter you pretend, my son's surges would be in decline, not climbing."

"Pretend?" she repeated, stunned by the venom in that single word. The heat in her chest climbed swiftly. She tried not to let her indignation show, but her voice trembled with the effort to keep it steady. "I have stabilized Taron's aura each time it threatened to flare beyond control. If you recall the farmland incident, it was my wards that prevented the entire orchard from catching fire."

Ulric waved a dismissive hand. It made her feel as though every success she'd labored to secure had been tossed aside like so much chaff. "You're here by my decree," he said, emphasizing each word. "Make no mistake, Cassandra, if Taron's magic continues to fracture like it has, and if another catastrophic surge befalls this barony, I will hold you fully responsible." He inclined his head, eyes glittering cold. "Do you understand?"

The flicker of torchlight illuminated the shock on the watchers' faces. Or perhaps it was fear, for no one wanted to be on the receiving end of Ulric's wrath. Cassandra's pulse pounded so violently that she feared they might see the blood rushing to her cheeks.

She recalled Taron's confession mere nights ago, the painful revelation that Ulric had once explicitly threatened Cassandra's life should Taron disobey him. How Taron had been coerced into silence while she was exiled. The memory flooded her mind now, fueling her with fresh outrage. How many times would Ulric exploit Taron's struggle for his own ends? For how long would he crush his son beneath that controlling fist?

The words poured out before she could stop them, sharper than the crack of Ulric's palm on the table. "If you truly cared about Taron, you'd be investigating this sabotage instead of twisting every failure into an indictment of me. You speak of his struggle, his instability, as if it's some weapon to wield rather than the consequence of a system you refuse to fix. *Taron* nearly died in that orchard, and what do you do? Use it as leverage to control your son—to control *us*."

The room's tension sharpened to a knife's edge, the nobles exchanging scandalized glances, but Cassandra didn't care. The low burn in her chest had erupted into an inferno. Her voice rose, steady and clear, cutting through the stunned silence like a blade. "I've done everything to protect him, *everything*, while you sit on your hands, blind to the danger that creeps closer every day. So, tell me, my lord—how many more times will you fail him? How many more times will you fail this barony before the consequences become irreversible?"

Ulric's glare darkened to pure menace, his lips pressing into a thin line, but Cassandra stepped forward, undeterred. Her hand gripped the back of a nearby chair, the wood groaning under her fingers as she leaned in, her gaze locking on his. "You can threaten me all you like," she said, voice dropping to a dangerous softness, "but don't mistake me for one of your cowed knights. I won't stand here and let you gamble with Taron's life—or mine—any longer."

Her words landed like hammer blows in the stillness, and for a moment, even Ulric seemed to hesitate, his cold fury meeting the unrelenting fire in her eyes.

Her words left the air electric. A startled murmur swept through the council. Across from her, a steward exchanged a wide-eyed glance with one of the noble councilors. Even the scribes paused mid-quill, jaws slack at the boldness of Cassandra's accusation. Catching a glimpse of Sir Barro, she saw his expression shift: half concern, half grudging admiration that she dared say it aloud.

Ulric's lips drew into a thin line. His knuckles turned white against the table's edge. "Take care, witch," he growled, voice resonating in the chamber's hush. "I will not have you stand here and presume to lecture me on my responsibilities to my own son. You claim sabotage is the real cause? Then find me proof that doesn't hinge on your word alone."

Anger seared through her. "I'm not disparaging your paternity, my lord, but it's no secret you've been prepared to wield Taron's power as leverage for your own ends. You used his surges once before to further your cause, exiling me to make certain he toed the line." The memory of Taron's anguished remorse, the quiet way he'd admitted letting her take the punishment, scratched at her composure. "And now, you'd do it again if it benefits you."

A collective inhale rippled around the room. She felt their stares, some scandalized, some disbelieving. No one dared interject. She was hurling a direct accusation at the baron.

Ulric's eyes burned with cold fury. "How dare you." The corners of his mouth twitched, and she realized he was barely maintaining his veneer of calm. "Your presence in this keep remains tenuous. Speak so disrespectfully again, and you may find yourself back in exile, or far worse. This time, I doubt I'd offer you the mercy of mere banishment."

For an instant, Cassandra's nerve wavered. A memory flickered: the day he had cast her from these walls, his sentence declared so final, so absolute. She remembered all too well how powerless she'd felt, how scornful the keep's courtiers had been, jeering at her downfall. That sense of injustice turned her dread into a burning resolve. She refused to yield. Not this time.

She forced herself to lift her chin. "Threaten me if you must," she said quietly. "But it won't change the fact that Taron's wards are being tampered with from within. And if you don't root out the culprit, you'll be condemning your own son to a fate you claim you want to prevent."

Ulric's eyes narrowed. He looked about to retort when the door behind the cluster of lesser knights scraped open. A sudden hush descended over the entire chamber. Cassandra's attention darted toward the newcomer, and her heart gave a jolting thud.

TEN

Taron stood at the threshold; one hand braced against the doorframe. He wore a tailored tunic of deep navy embroidered with subdued runic lines around the cuffs, insignias designed to help manage minor fluctuations in his aura. Gaze flicking across the room, he took in the tension like a man stumbling into a battlefield. There was weariness in the set of his shoulders, but also a coil of tension that declared he was far from beaten.

He locked eyes with Cassandra first. The flicker of his expression, part regret, part something akin to encouragement, nearly stole her breath. She could guess the swirl of emotions he felt, walking in to see her locked in a verbal duel with his father. Anxiety and guilt, yes, but also a fiercely protective glint that made her chest tighten.

Then Taron clenched his jaw and turned to face Ulric. "Father," he said, his voice careful. "I heard your summons demanded Cassandra's presence. I gathered that it might... concern me as well."

Ulric's glare pinned Taron. "This meeting is not about you. It's about her failings in containing your surges."

"I think it's both," Taron replied, a trace of defiance in his tone. He took a few steps forward, ignoring how half the onlooking council stiffened at his approach, as though expecting magical sparks to arc off him at any second. "Everyone here knows I'm the one living with these surges. We also know Cassandra has prevented them from becoming outright catastrophes more times than any prior warder."

A murmured hush spread. Some heads nodded faintly, especially among the lesser knights who had witnessed Cassandra's interventions firsthand. Cassandra's pulse sang with a complicated mix of gratitude and dread. That Taron dared speak up in open defiance of his father was no small thing, but it also put him at risk of Ulric's notorious wrath.

The baron's gaze shifted, ice in every line of his face. "Taron," he said softly, in that clipped voice that carried the weight of paternal condemnation. "We will discuss your part in this privately. For now, Cassandra must be reminded of her responsibility, one she has yet to fulfill."

Ulric leaned back in his chair; his expression tight with irritation. "The matter of her competence is not for you to determine, Taron. This is a council matter, and you would do well to remember your place."

Taron's jaw tightened, and for a moment, Cassandra thought he might back down. But instead, he stepped closer to the table, his hands braced on its edge as he leaned forward to meet his father's gaze. "My place," he said evenly, though his voice carried a sharp edge, "is here. And it's my magic at risk, my life Cassandra has saved time and again. You can't dismiss that, no matter how much you wish to."

The baron's eyes narrowed. "You think this is about wishing? About dismissing? This is about the survival of this barony. And if your so-called ward-crafter—"

"Enough," Taron interrupted, his voice rising just enough to cut through his father's tirade. The council shifted uncomfortably, murmurs rippling through the room. Taron straightened, his shoulders squared and turned to face the gathered nobles and stewards. "If anyone here doubts Cassandra's loyalty or her abilities, let me remind you of the countless times she's stabilized my surges, protected this land, and prevented disasters that would have been far worse if not for her."

Ulric's face darkened, but Taron pressed on, his voice unwavering. "Yes, I've struggled to control my magic, but that's not because of Cassandra. It's because of the sabotage she's been tirelessly working to uncover while you," he turned back to his father, "stand by and accuse her instead of the real culprits. If you want someone to blame, blame the saboteurs, not the person holding everything together."

A heavy silence fell over the room, broken only by the faint scrape of a chair as one of the councilors shifted uncomfortably.

Ulric's gaze turned glacial. "And what would you have me do, Taron? Entrust the entire barony's future to a witch exiled for—"

"I would have you trust me," Taron said, cutting him off once more. "Trust my judgment, trust my experience. And trust that I will not abandon Cassandra again."

The words hung in the air; a declaration heavier than anything else spoken that day. Cassandra's breath caught, her gaze snapping to Taron. His eyes burned with a fierce intensity, one that made her chest ache with a mixture of hope and disbelief.

Ulric rose slowly, his chair scraping against the floor as he loomed over the table. "You presume to lecture me, boy?" His voice dropped, dangerously low. "You think you can dictate who belongs in this keep, who I should trust? You forget yourself."

"No," Taron said firmly, his hands clenching into fists at his sides. "For years, I let you dictate my choices. I let you manipulate me, force me to push away the one person who's always been in my corner. That ends now. You can dismiss me, call me a boy if it makes you feel powerful, but I'm not backing down. Cassandra stays, and I'll make sure she has everything she needs to find the truth and protect this barony.

Ulric stared him down, but Taron didn't flinch. The tension in the room was palpable, as though the very air held its breath.

"And if you're going to threaten her again," Taron added, his voice low but steel-edged, "know that you'll have to go through me first."

Cassandra felt her heart pounding in her chest, the sheer weight of Taron's words crashing over her. She had spent so long bracing for hostility, for blame, that this open, public defense left her almost unmoored. She had to speak. "My lord baron, I've never once turned my back on Taron's condition. Day in and day out, I do everything possible to keep him from falling into another meltdown. But that alone won't suffice if the sabotage continues." She refused to make eye contact with Ulric. "You demanded I anchor him. I've done so. Don't blame me if someone is deliberately loosening the supports from the shadows."

A strangled hush followed. Cassandra realized, with a kind of detached clarity, that a lesser person in her position might have buckled under the baron's scorn. But she was done cowering. She let her anger and her sense of injustice fortify her stance.

Ulric drummed his fingers on the tabletop, the only outward sign of his frustration. "You speak incessantly of sabotage, yet you cannot name a single conspirator. You prattle on about forged ledgers, yet you cannot identify who penned them. With no culprit to present, how can you expect me to accept your word as truth?"

Cassandra's temples throbbed. "I'm not finished gathering evidence," she answered. "Some knights have glimpsed figures in the orchard, or by the storerooms, always at odd hours. Sir Barro himself has begun verifying,"

"Sir Barro is my knight, not yours," Ulric snapped. "He is free to investigate as he pleases, but that does not exonerate you."

She glanced Barro's way, noticing how his mouth pressed into a taut line. He offered the barest inclination of his head, acknowledgment that mirrored Cassandra's words. But apparently, he dared not speak openly in her defense with so many councilors present. She couldn't blame him for his caution, though frustration gnawed at her anew.

Ulric rose to his feet in a single fluid motion. The tension in the chamber multiplied, like a rolling thundercloud about to spill lightning. "Let me be clear," he said, voice low, "I see no progress in reining Taron's aura. None. My son is still dangerously unstable. The farmland wards flicker every few nights. And the restless talk among commonfolk erodes confidence in this keep. They whisper that Taron's next surge will decimate entire villages." He paused, letting that threat hang. "If you fail to show tangible improvement, an end to these surges, I will see you removed, Cassandra. This time, permanently."

A wave of fury threatened to clog her throat. She scarcely felt Taron's quick gaze flick in her direction, a near-silent plea for caution. Memories of Taron's forced silence in her past hearing crashed against her reason. She imagined him as a young man trembling on the cusp of speaking out, only for Ulric's threats to chain him. That was the same tactic the baron was using on her now. The same tactic that had cost her so many years in exile.

She found she could not remain silent. "You'll see me removed to hide your own failings," she said, each syllable trembling with quiet wrath. "Because if you admit sabotage is real, then you must concede that Taron's condition isn't my sole responsibility. You, as the baron, would need to reorganize your knights, your resources, your entire approach. And the blame might come resting at your feet."

A scandalized gasp skittered along the council table. Ulric's nostrils flared. He looked perilously close to launching a full tirade, but for once, Cassandra refused to let him speak first.

"You want accelerated warding solutions?" she continued, voice rising. She turned a fraction, sweeping her gaze over the wide-eyed stewards, the minor lords, the scribes. "Then allow me to do my work unimpeded. Stop feeding these rumors that I sabotage Taron. Stop ignoring the forged ledgers. Let me, and the knights who believe me, run a proper investigation. Otherwise, there will be no progress."

Ulric's open hand slammed down again, and the wooden table shuddered. "Witch," he spat, "do you truly dare to presume authority in my keep? You have no rank, no standing. You remain here at my sufferance. Or do you fancy yourself baroness?" A nasty twist laced his words. "Perhaps you think your closeness to my son grants you license to speak above your station."

She felt the weight of Taron's presence, how he bristled at the insinuation that her only influence came from a would-be romantic link. Heat flushed her cheeks, half from indignation, half from the flicker of guilt and longing that always spiked when she thought about how Taron and she once felt about each other. She was aware of the scrutiny from every corner of the hall, of the speculative looks swirling at the mention of her "closeness."

"As if you haven't used Taron for your own ends," she

fired back, ignoring the scandalized hiss of one of the councilors. "This time, I won't stand by while you warp the truth. Taron's safety, indeed, this entire barony's safety, demands acknowledging the real threat." Summoning what poise she could muster, she added, "And if you want me to protect him, you'll let me do it in the way I see fit."

Taron stepped forward; his expression knotted with tension. "Father, we have to."

Ulric's glare turned on him, cold and biting. "Silence," he barked. "I have indulged your outbursts far too often these past weeks. If you had any sense—"

Taron's anger ignited like a flame catching oil, and the air in the chamber thickened as his magic surged. The faint glow around his aura brightened, pulsing in time with his rising fury. His hands clenched into fists at his sides, and for a brief moment, the council chamber felt like it might collapse under the pressure.

"No," Taron said, his voice steady and forceful, cutting off his father mid-sentence. "I won't stay silent this time." His words carried an edge of raw power, his magic crackling in the air like a brewing storm.The room fell deathly still, every councilor and steward freezing in place as the weight of Taron's presence grew. Ulric stepped back instinctively, his composure faltering for the first time as a tendril of heat rippled through the air and licked dangerously close to him.

Taron took a deliberate step forward, his magic radiating from him in waves. "You don't get to threaten Cassandra anymore," he said, his voice low but filled with unmistakable authority. "You don't get to dismiss the truth, ignore the sabotage, or use my surges as an excuse to control everyone around you."

Ulric's eyes narrowed, but his face had lost some of its color. "Taron, enough of this—"

"No," Taron snapped, the force of his words sending another ripple of energy through the room. This time, the flicker of heat was undeniable, and Ulric stumbled back a step, his hand gripping the edge of the table as if to steady himself. "You've spent your life controlling everyone—me, Cassandra, this entire council. But I'm done letting you use me to enforce your will."

The council chamber was silent except for the faint crackle of Taron's magic, which seemed to hum with his fury. Even the knights standing guard had taken a step back, their hands hovering near their weapons, though none dared draw them.

Taron's gaze locked onto his father's, unflinching. "You think I don't remember how you forced me to stay silent when you exiled Cassandra? How did you make me watch while you destroyed the one person who was willing to stand by me when my magic threatened to consume me? You've used threats and fear to control me for too long, but not anymore."

Cassandra stared at him, her heart pounding as she saw the sheer conviction in his eyes. This wasn't the hesitant, guilt-ridden Taron she'd known before. This was a man who had finally broken free of his father's chains, standing unshaken in the face of the baron's wrath.

Ulric's voice, when it came, was strained, a veneer of

authority stretched thin. "You would turn your back on your family, your duty, for her?"

"For her, for me, for this barony," Taron said, his voice rising with a sharpness that cut through the room like a blade. "Because if you don't see the truth now, if you don't let Cassandra do what needs to be done, then this keep, this land, will crumble under the weight of your pride."

ELEVEN

The baron's lips curled, but before he could retort, Taron took another step forward, his magic flaring again. The heat was intense now, brushing the edge of Ulric's doublet, close enough that the faint scent of singed fabric filled the air. The baron recoiled slightly, his face pale, his control slipping.

"I'm not afraid of you anymore," Taron said, his voice quiet but resonating with power. "And you'll never make me abandon Cassandra again. If you try, you'll see just how far I'll go to protect her."

Ulric's mouth opened, but no words came. He looked at his son as though seeing him for the first time, not as the boy he had controlled, but as a man who would no longer be bent to his will.

The room was frozen, the councilors and stewards staring wide-eyed at the scene unfolding before them. Even Cassandra felt rooted in place, her heart racing as she watched Taron confront his father with a strength she hadn't dared hope he would find.

Finally, Ulric straightened, regaining a measure of composure, though his face remained tense. "Very well," he said stiffly, his voice cold and clipped. "If you're so insistent, Taron, then the responsibility is yours. But mark my words, any failure will be on your head."

Taron didn't flinch. He simply inclined his head, his gaze never leaving his father's. "I'll take that risk."

Ulric turned abruptly, his cloak sweeping behind him as he strode from the chamber without another word. The councilors exchanged nervous glances but remained silent, clearly unwilling to cross either Taron or his father.

Cassandra knew that no matter what she said, the baron would keep twisting her attempts into perceived failures.

She inhaled a shaking breath, let it fill her lungs, then snapped her gaze around the table. The hush weighed heavily. She could taste the tension on her tongue. Slowly, with deliberate steps, she turned from her place near the center.

Ulric's commanding presence glowered behind her, but she refused to cringe away. She deserved more than these veiled and outright threats. "I won't bow to your intimidation," she said, each syllable carrying defiant calm. "Taron's surges are not a game for you to manipulate, my lord. You may hold the barony in your grip, but I assure you, you won't break me a second time."

She caught a final glimpse of Taron. Their eyes met in a fleeting moment of intensity, his swirling with silent apology, hers with unrelenting determination. The savage glare in Ulric's gaze warned her not to speak further. Her heart hammered so loudly that she nearly missed the hush that fell among the watchers.

Ulric's glare darkened, his expression a storm cloud of suppressed fury. "Watch your tongue, witch," he growled, the venom in his tone enough to make even the bravest councilor avert their gaze.

But Cassandra held her ground, the fiery resolve in her eyes meeting his unflinchingly. Her chest heaved with the effort of keeping her composure, her magic swirling just beneath the surface of her skin like an untamed current. Every instinct screamed at her to lash out, to shove his arrogance and cruelty back in his face. It would be so easy —just one slip, one flare of power, and she could make him understand the weight of his threats.

The thought was tempting, dangerously so.

Then she caught Taron's gaze. His eyes, blazing with anger and something deeper—protective, unyielding— locked onto hers. There was no apology in them now, only a fierce determination that mirrored her own. He was with her, she realized, not just in words but in spirit.

But that wasn't enough to quell the tempest inside her. Her hands itched, fingers curling and uncurling as she fought to keep her power in check. If she stayed here any longer, she knew she would lose control. Not over her magic—she could rein that in. But over herself. Over the fury that threatened to explode and reduce Baron Ulric's smug composure to ash.

She couldn't give him that satisfaction.

Without another word, Cassandra turned on her heel. The sharp echo of her footfalls cut through the silence like the crack of a whip, each step a declaration of her refusal to yield. Her back straight, her chin high, she strode toward the door, the weight of every gaze in the room pressing against her.

The murmurs began as she neared the threshold, faint at first but growing louder. She could feel the mix of emotions swirling in the room—shock, dismay, grudging respect, and fear. Let them wonder. Let them doubt. She wouldn't waste her breath explaining herself to men and women who would never understand the battle she was fighting.

Her fingers gripped the heavy iron handle of the chamber door, and for a moment, she paused. The whispers behind her faded into a tense stillness.

She didn't look back. "You can threaten me all you like, my lord," she said, her voice calm but cutting, carrying effortlessly across the room. "But you should be more concerned about the enemies inside your walls. You might find they're not so easily dismissed."

With that, she pushed the door open, letting it swing shut behind her with a resounding thud. The sound reverberated through the chamber like the closing of a coffin lid, and for a fleeting moment, Cassandra felt as though she'd sealed something behind her, something dangerous, volatile, and ready to ignite.

The anger still churned in her chest, hot and wild,

threatening to consume her if she didn't release it soon. The thought of Ulric's sneer, his condescension, his blatant disregard for the truth—every piece of it fueled the fire inside her.

Without another word, she strode away, footfalls echoing sharply against the stone floor. A murmur rippled behind her as she neared the door, and she sensed every eye in the chamber pinned to her retreating figure: some in shock, some in dismay, and more than a few in grudging respect at the nerve she'd just displayed.

The vaulted corridor beyond was blessedly cooler, a rush of air that carried the scents of tallow wax and old tapestries. She stalked it down, her breath coming fast, her hands still clenched. Her blood throbbed in her ears. The weight of that confrontation pressed on her ribs like a vise, but a fierce sense of triumph warred with her anger. She had refused to let Ulric corner her, refused to let him trample her under accusations she hadn't earned.

Tense knights, posted outside, swiveled their heads as she strode past. Behind the closed double doors, she could still hear the low rumble of Baron Ulric's voice, presumably continuing the meeting in her absence. Or perhaps venting his frustration upon Taron, who had dared to speak up. Concern for Taron jabbed at her, but she swallowed it down. She couldn't remain in that stifling chamber any longer without risking her own composure.

She passed a wide pillar braced by a decorative tapestry and had to pause for a moment, leaning against the cold stone. Her heart felt like it might burst through her ribs. She replayed the baron's threat in her mind: If Taron's next surge is not contained, if the farmland wards flicker, if sabotage intensifies...she would bear the punishment. That vow glinted like a blade in the darkness.

TWELVE

A wave of old dread rose conjuring visions of how easily he'd exiled her once. She shook it off. She couldn't let fear hobble her now. Taron needed her, even if his father wanted to spin it as though she were the cause of all that had gone wrong. She wasn't powerless this time, not with the partial evidence she and Sir Barro had gathered, not with Taron's quiet willingness to stand with her. For all his father's intimidation, Taron had offered her those desperate words of support. And that, at least, gave her a sliver of hope.

But no matter how much hope she clung to, the baron had made one point clear: he would not let her presence subvert his will. He would cling to the narrative that she was failing at her job. And if Taron's magic spasmed again, the baron would move against her in a far harsher way than simply an open threat in front of the council.

Fine, she thought, stepping away from the pillar. Let

him try. She still had something she lacked all those years ago: knowledge, allies, knights who had seen the sabotage marks with their own eyes. She refused to be a scapegoat. She refused to let Taron break under his father's manipulations. Gathering a shaking breath, she thrust her shoulders back, forcing her posture upright as she marched deeper into the corridor.

Distantly, she heard footsteps and hushes, but none belonged to Taron. She guessed he was still inside, forced to face Ulric's wrath alone. Anger curled inside her once more. She had left him behind in that pit of tension, but the alternative, remaining and letting her rage at Ulric morph into something neither she nor Taron could control, would have done no good.

A swirl of conflicting emotions threatened to drag her under: frustration that no matter how plainly she spoke, the baron refused to budge; fear that Taron's next surge might push both of them over the brink in Ulric's eyes; and a fierce, blazing determination that sabotage or not, she would fight to protect Taron from the worst of the baron's cruelty.

Lost in that whirlwind, she barely noticed the pairs of passing knights who pressed themselves to the walls, giving her an uncommonly wide berth. She realized they must have recognized her expression or perhaps overheard some muffled snippet of her confrontation. Let them stare, she thought savagely. She was done hiding. If something monstrous reared its head in the keep again, like those suspicious rods or forged ledgers, she would expose it. She would drag the sabotage into the light if it killed her.

She reached the corridor's far archway, bursting into a smaller side hall that branched toward the main staircase. The heavy hush of the keep enclosed her. Fury still pulsed at the edges of her vision. Her breath ragged, she replayed her last words to the baron. They felt both terrifying and strangely liberating. She had told him off. Had stood her ground. That would come with consequences, and yet, for the first time, she truly felt that she had seized a fragment of her lost agency.

Small, quick footsteps rushed from behind, and she turned to spot a wide-eyed page half bowing, half stumbling to keep pace with her strides. "M-Mistress Cassandra," the boy murmured, looking anxious.

She forced her expression to soften slightly, none of this was the child's fault. "Yes?"

"The baron...they, I heard shouting. Are you,"

She cut him off with a small shake of her head. "I'm fine," she said firmly, rummaging for composure. "No message to deliver, I presume?"

"No, mistress," he stammered. "I only...well, they all seemed so angry, and I heard rumors you,"

"Tell them whatever they like," she said, her tone more clipped than she intended. "I have nothing further to say. Now excuse me." The boy lurched backward, startled by her abruptness. Cassandra inhaled and reined in her frustration. "Apologies," she offered more gently. "I've had a difficult morning." She left the page behind, continuing down the hallway before he could snare her in more queries.

Sconces blurred as she descended a winding flight of stairs. The stone steps were cold beneath her feet, each scuffle of her shoes echoing the last. The keep felt both suffocating and deserted at once, a place of secrets that refused to breathe. But that confrontation had changed something in her. She could almost feel a new clarity forging inside her. No matter how Ulric tried to corner or threaten her, she wouldn't step back into the role of the scapegoat. She had Taron's welfare at heart, had repeatedly saved him from the brink, and would do so again. She might not wear a noble's crest or hold recognized authority, but she would fight for him, and for herself.

She reached the base of the stairs, the main corridor stretching ahead. From there, she could head toward the keep's library, or the courtyard, or even Taron's chamber. The swirl of unspent rage and cold adrenaline still coursed through her, making every muscle buzz with tension. She pictured Taron's stricken face, how he'd arrived mid-lash, how his father's savage glare warned him to stay silent. Her heart twisted in frustration. He had tried, but old patterns ran deep. Ulric could browbeat Taron into retreat with shocking ease.

No more. She remembered the vow Taron had made to her in quieter moments, promising not to let her face his father alone. And she recalled her own vow not to let Taron suffer under sabotage or paternal oppression. The baron might last out, might threaten her with dire consequences, but if Taron faced another magical crisis, she would be at his side no matter what.

For now, she needed to breathe, needed to let the flames of her anger recede. She needed a moment to gather her composure, to decide how best to proceed with the sabotage investigation under these tight constraints. Because if she truly hoped to exonerate herself, prove the sabotage was real, silence the baron's accusations once and for all, then she had work to do. She would need to coordinate with Sir Barro more carefully, gather statements from the orchard guards, intercept the next suspicious crate before it vanished. She had no illusions that it would be easy.

But she had not come all this way, had not braved the baron's hostility, nor Taron's swirling aura, nor the keep's malice, just to bow her head and let the blame bury her. She was done letting fear throttle her voice. She was Cassandra, a witch with warding power that had already saved lives, and she'd face worse than an arrogant baron to protect Taron and, by extension, this entire barony.

Bolstering herself with that reminder, she started down the corridor with renewed purpose. Behind her, the council chamber door remained firmly shut, the resonance of Baron Ulric's tirade muffled beyond the stone. That was fine. Let him rant. Let him rage. She had made her position undeniably clear.

And as she marched away from that seat of power, her heartbeat vibrated with a fierce mixture of vindication and fury, her vow echoing in every step. None in that hall could doubt her resolve now. No matter what doom Ulric threatened, she refused to be a pawn ever again.

She quickened her pace, shoulders taut with the after-shock of conflict, but back unbowed, her eyes already scanning for the next point of action. Because indeed, if there had been any doubt of her resolve, it was gone, gone, like smoke curling in the morning breeze.

THIRTEEN

Cassandra's eyes snapped open sometime past midnight, her heart thrumming with the unnerving sense that something was terribly wrong. For a confused instant, in the darkness of her cramped chamber, she thought she'd only drifted into another uneasy dream. But then she heard it, a thunderous pounding on her door, forceful enough to shake the hinges. Her pulse accelerated, dread coiling through her belly as she struggled free of tangled blankets.

"Open up!" A guard's voice, muffled but insistent, cut through the hush of the keep's sleeping corridors. "Hurry, Mistress Cassandra, he's surging!"

Taron.

Shoving her tangled hair behind her shoulders, she sprang from the narrow bed, fumbling for the shawl draped over a trunk. Her legs trembled as she recalled how only hours before, he had come to her with a deeply worried expression, muttering about fresh sabotage near his quarters. Someone had tampered with the wards in the corridor outside Taron's chamber and scrawled incomplete runes to coax his magic into another violent spiral. At the time, she and Sir Barro had done what they could, scraping away the worst of those runes and quietly re-etching protective wards to hold Taron's aura steady. But they must have missed something...or a secondary trick lay in wait.

No time to question it now. She wrenched the door open, face to face with two breathless guards. One was the sandy-haired young sentinel she had seen in passing during orchard patrols; the other, older, with flinty eyes. Both were wide-eyed with fear. Even the older guard looked ready to bolt.

"He's in the corridor outside his chambers," the sandy-haired guard said hurriedly, not waiting for formality. "There's, light, sparks, like he'll burn everything if we don't contain it."

Cassandra felt her lungs tighten. "Where is Sir Barro?" she asked, voice rough from lack of sleep.

"Barro's gone to gather reinforcements," said the flinty-eyed guard. "But he told us to fetch you straight away."

"Then we go now." She pulled the shawl taut against her shoulders, not bothering with proper shoes; she only shoved her feet into soft slippers. Her belt pouch hung from a hook by the door. She snatched it, double-checking her coil of warding chalk inside. Heart hammering, she followed the guards into the corridor.

The moment she stepped into the hall, a wave of

prickling energy prickled her skin. It was as though the very stones underfoot vibrated with Taron's power. The torches flickering in their sconces seemed dimmer than usual, dwarfed by the glow up ahead, a searing, pale light that spilled into the hallway from around the nearest turn.

She pushed forward, ignoring the startled looks of a few servants who peered out from doorways, nightcaps askew. Their fear was palpable. She couldn't blame them: Taron's power, unleashed, was no gentle thing.

"Stay back," she ordered the guards as they approached the final length of corridor. "I don't know how bad it is."

The flinty-eyed guard nodded, relief showing in his posture. "We'll hold the rest of the keep at bay," he muttered. "Just, try to help him."

Cassandra took a breath she did not feel, then slipped around the bend. At once, her vision flooded with brilliant arcs of supernatural light. Silver and pale blue energy crackled along the walls, licking over stone in fits of violent sparks. A painting had fallen from its hook and lay half-scorched on the floor, edges curling in black. The tapestries covering the corridor's far wall fluttered in an unseen gale, whipped by raw magical force. She could hardly see Taron at first for the blinding swirl backlighting him.

"Taron!" she called, voice vibrating in her throat. Squinting against the glare, she spotted him standing near a small wooden table, though "standing" was a generous description. His back was hunched, his head bowed, as if he could barely remain upright. Sparks arced off him in wild bursts, ricocheting down the hall.

He didn't seem to hear her. The black hair she'd last seen neatly brushed back now hung loose across his forehead, plastered with sweat. She smelled the pungent singe of overheated magic, reminiscent of ozone and burnt cloth. The entire corridor felt stifling, the air was thick and charged with unbridled energy.

Cassandra exhaled, steeling herself to approach. She carefully lifted her hands in front of her, letting the soft glow of her own warding power gather at her fingertips. Despite her clanging nerves, she forced herself forward step by step, as if moving through a violent gust of wind. Perhaps no one else dared come closer lest one of Taron's arcs lash out and sear them. She swallowed down a spike of fear. She had faced his surges before. She knew how to anchor him, better than anyone.

"Taron!" she shouted again, voice raw. "Look at me!"

A fresh burst of energy crackled around him, lighting up the corridor. She glimpsed shriveled bits of half-scraped runes scrawled on the nearby wall, those sabotage markings they'd tried to remove earlier. Something must have reactivated them. Gritting her teeth, Cassandra reached into her belt pouch, fumbling for the piece of warding chalk that gave off a faint herbal tang. Even as she tried to concentrate, another crack of power pulsed from Taron's body, rattling the stone. She staggered, bracing herself against the wall for support.

"Taron," she said, more softly this time. The corridor

roiled with his magic, but she pressed on, ignoring the risk. She wouldn't let him drown in this, not again.

At last, his head jerked up, eyes half-wild. Sparks danced across his gaze in swirling flecks of hazel and white light. The retort of arcane energy sent tremors through the walls, as if the keep itself shuddered with each of his ragged breaths.

"Cassandra..." he managed, voice tight with pain. His legs nearly buckled. She lunged, reaching him just in time to steady his arm. This close, the crackling magic made every hair on her body lift, like a storm about to break. His forearm felt hot to the touch, almost too hot, but she refused to let go. This was Taron, the man who never wanted his power to harm anyone.

She pressed one hand flat to his chest, the other bracing around his back. The swirl of magic surged in protest, scorching her palm with tingling sparks. A hiss escaped her lips, but she gathered her courage and inhaled, focusing on the old techniques Miriana had taught her for anchoring volatile energy.

"Stay with me," she whispered, feeling him quake against her body. "I'm going to siphon off what I can. Just...hold on."

He made a sound somewhere between a groan and a gasp, whether in pain or relief, she couldn't tell. She closed her eyes, letting her healing sense wander through the scorching aura that enveloped him. His wards, always faintly visible to her inner sight, looked jagged now, all the runic patterns twisted out of alignment. Where sabotage runes had scuffed at the edges, the blowback only grew more ferocious.

Cassandra angled her body, in part to shield Taron from the corridor behind her, he was beyond seeing reason, and she needed a stable vantage. With trembling fingers, she drew swift, sure strokes of chalk across the back of his hand, weaving a short, emergency ward designed to quell immediate magical surges.

The moment the chalk's faint glow lit up, Taron gasped, a fresh wave of crackling power sparking around his torso. "I, can't..." he grated out, voice hoarse. "It's... pulling too hard. Feels like it's ripping me apart."

"Shh," she murmured, keeping her voice level though her heart hammered. "I'll catch you."

She reached deeper with her healing magic, forging a link to Taron's aura. Warmth cascaded from her chest down her arms, tingling at her fingertips where she pressed against him. His ragged breathing echoed in her ears. The corridor quaked again, dust sifting from the overhead rafters. Somewhere behind them, she heard distant shouts, guards, maybe even servants, but all she could focus on was Taron's frantic heartbeat pulsing under her hand.

FOURTEEN

The synergy they shared, something no other warder had fully managed, flickered to life. She felt his chaotic magic surge into her, as if molten power poured through a narrow channel between them. For a dizzying moment, the pain was blinding; she bit back a cry, bracing her stance to avoid collapsing. But Miriana's teachings came back in a wave, reminding her to let the energy pass through, not to fight it. Slowly, she guided that molten surge along the invisible lines of the ward she'd drawn on Taron's skin, allowing it to bleed off into the stone floor at her feet. A swirl of pale green and silver flared across her forearms in ghostly patterns, the sign that her siphoning had begun.

Taron's fingers curled into her shoulders as he clung to her. She felt the rigid tension in his body, every muscle tight with the strain of containing power that rebelled at every turn. Another crackle soared down the corridor, this time away from them, smashing into a tapestry. The cloth instantly burst into flames. Cassandra's eyes flew open at the sudden blaze, but she forced herself not to panic; if she broke contact with Taron now, the next surge could be deadly.

"Cassandra," he choked out, pressing his forehead against her temple.

"I'm all right," she lied. Truly, her nerves were shot, and her heart hammered painfully. She had to end this soon or else put them both in greater peril. "Just focus on me. Let your power come to me."

He nodded jerkily against her, arms trembling as he tried to guide the flow. Her senses reeled with the intensity of his magic swirling across her body, making her own wards flicker in a fiery dance of synergy. For a wild instant, she caught the faint scent of Taron's sweat and the musky tang of scorching energy, both mixing into a heady, electric aroma. In that swirl of heat and power, the world felt dangerously small, just the two of them pinned together under the burden of his unstoppable magic.

Nearby, the burning tapestry crackled. She could hear a guard's panicked shout. But she had to stay locked on Taron, forging that delicate bridge that would keep him from succumbing. Another wave of magic surged through him, so violent her knees almost buckled. She bore down, inhaling steady, letting her own aura expand, weaving fresh threads of calm that might anchor him.

"It's you," he managed, voice a fervent rasp against her cheek. "You're the only one who, makes it stop."

His words, jagged and raw, sank into her heart. Part of her flinched at the reminder that no other warder had taken his place, that he'd needed her all along. The bitterness over her exile, the swirl of heartbreak, she could feel it flicker inside her, but she pushed it aside for now. They had no space for old wounds in this moment; Taron's life was at stake.

She forced a steadiness into her voice. "Then hold on to me. Don't let go."

Their bodies nearly melded together with the force of the next surge. She clutched him tight, ignoring the scorching sting.

Cassandra could feel the unsteady rhythm of Taron's heartbeat beneath her palm, thundering against her hand as if desperate to break free. She didn't loosen her grip on him, not yet, not while she could still feel the faintest flicker of energy rippling under his skin. Her runes glimmered softly now, no longer burning with the frenzied chaos they had just contained, and the room was steeped in a quiet that felt fragile, like the moment before glass shattered.

"Taron," she whispered again, her voice raw with exhaustion and something deeper, something she hadn't allowed herself to name until now. "Look at me."

Slowly, his eyes fluttered open, their stormy depths meeting hers with a vulnerability that stole her breath. The wildness was gone, replaced by a heavy weariness, but there was something else, too—gratitude, longing, and the kind of trust that made her chest tighten. She traced the edge of his jaw with her fingertips, the motion unhurried and tender, and his breath hitched in response.

"I'm here," she said softly, her voice a balm against the tension still coiled in his body. "I'm not going anywhere."

Taron's hands came up to cradle her face, his touch gentle yet sure, as though grounding himself through her. "You saved me," he murmured, his voice thick with emotion. "Again."

Her lips curved faintly, though her heart ached at the weight of his words. "You don't need saving, Taron. You need someone who believes in you. And I do."

His thumb brushed over her cheek, lingering on the line of her jaw, and the spark in his gaze shifted, deepening into something that sent a shiver through her. "Cassandra," he said, her name a quiet plea on his lips, and before she could respond, he kissed her.

It wasn't frantic or desperate, but deliberate, his lips moving against hers with a certainty that made her knees weak. She melted into him, her hands sliding up his chest to anchor herself as their kiss deepened, slow and all-encompassing. Every brush of his lips, every gentle graze of his teeth, seemed to draw the lingering tension from her, leaving only a warmth that curled low in her belly and spread outward.

Taron's hands left her face to trail down her shoulders, his touch reverent and unhurried as though memorizing every curve and hollow. His fingers found the ties of her tunic, loosening them with care, and Cassandra let out a soft sigh as the fabric slipped from her shoulders, pooling at their feet. Her own hands moved of their own accord, pulling at the fastenings of his tunic until she could slide it off him, baring the taut planes of his chest.

She leaned forward, pressing her lips to his collarbone, trailing kisses along the line of his throat and the hollow of his shoulder. Taron's breath hitched, his hands tightening on her hips as she pressed closer. "You don't know what you do to me," he murmured, his voice a low rumble that sent a thrill through her.

"Show me," she whispered, her voice steady despite the way her heart raced.

He did. His hands roamed her body, mapping every inch of her skin with a touch that was both possessive and tender. When his lips found hers again, the kiss was hungrier, deeper, and it consumed her. She felt the heat of his body against hers, the strength in his arms as he held her close, and the quiet hum of his magic pulsing just beneath the surface.

Cassandra's fingers tangled in his hair as he kissed down the curve of her neck, his mouth leaving a trail of fire in its wake. Her breath hitched when his lips found the hollow of her throat, and a quiet gasp escaped her when his hands cupped her waist, pulling her flush against him.

Their movements grew more urgent, the last remnants of distance between them disappearing as they came together. Every touch, every kiss, felt like a vow—a promise that neither of them would face the world alone again. She moved with him, her body attuned to his, and the tension that had once held them both captive unraveled in a crescendo of shared release.

Afterward, they lay tangled together on the floor, their breathing still uneven as the heat of their bodies slowly gave way to the cool air of the room. Cassandra rested her head against Taron's chest, her fingers tracing idle patterns over his skin. She could feel the steady rhythm of his heart, strong and sure, and the faint hum of his magic —a soft, pulsing glow instead of the violent storm it had been before.

He ran his fingers through her hair, his touch gentle. "Cassandra," he said quietly, his voice filled with awe, "it's... different. My magic. It feels steadier, more—" He paused, searching for the word. "Grounded."

She lifted her head to look at him, her brow furrowing slightly. "Do you think...?"

Taron nodded; his expression thoughtful. "When we were together just now, it felt like... like the chaos receded. Like I could control it." He cupped her cheek, his thumb brushing over her skin. "You calm the storm, Cassandra. You make me stronger."

Her chest tightened at the sincerity in his voice, and she leaned into his touch. "Maybe it's not just me," she said softly. "Maybe it's us. Together."

He smiled then, a rare, unguarded smile that lit up his face and made her heart flutter. "Then we'll face it together," he said, his voice steady and sure. "Whatever comes, I'm not letting go of this. Of you."

She pressed a kiss to his palm, her own resolve matching his. "Neither am I."

FIFTEEN

er lashes felt damp, whether from sweat or tears, she wasn't sure. Yet the worst of the chaos was beginning to ebb; she could sense it. The biting arcs of light that danced around Taron like a frenzied storm glimmered less intently, no longer snapping against the air with the same deadly force. A sheen of sweat slicked Cassandra's brow, and her breath came fast, but she refused to break contact until she felt him steady.

Their surroundings flickered, the corridor's shadows dancing as the intensity of Taron's surges gradually diminished. She felt the slow, deliberate intake of his breath against her collarbone, each inhale a shade less frantic than the last. The stone beneath her feet was hot but no longer shaking with violent tremors.

Head spinning, she exhaled in a trembling rush. "Taron," she whispered, voice shaking. "Open your eyes."

She felt his chest heave. Then, in the faint light of

surviving torches, his gaze flicked up to meet hers. Gone was that vacant, wild stare. In its place, she saw an exhausted, hollow relief. For a moment, neither of them spoke; the only sounds were their stuttering breaths and the distant hiss of smoldering fabric.

"You're safe," she managed, her words almost lost amid the hush that followed. She had to say it, if only to convince herself.

The shuddering aftershock of his magic coursed along his body, but she sensed that the worst of the meltdown had passed. The sabotage runes that had battered his aura were now scorched beyond any function, blackened shadows on the stone. Only the faint remnants of Cassandra's newly drawn wards glowed with residual power, pulsing softly at their feet.

He murmured something she couldn't catch. Carefully, she tilted her head to better see him. The flickering light revealed sweat beading along his temple, strands of dark hair sticking to his skin. The raw vulnerability in his eyes nearly undid her. It struck her with dreadful clarity that she'd never seen him look so helpless, so completely reliant on her.

"Cassandra," he whispered again, voice thick with exhaustion or perhaps gratitude; she could not say. His free hand lifted, trembling, unsteady, and curled lightly around the back of her neck. In that fleeting contact, they exchanged a thousand unspoken confessions.

Her heart lurched. She counted every breath, every quake in his limbs as he leaned on her. Warmth rippled across her chest, not entirely from his diminishing magic. "Are you in pain?" she asked softly, half-dreading the answer.

His eyes fluttered shut. "Less now," he managed. "Your wards...they help. You help."

She swallowed, her throat tightening. For an instant, her guard came crashing down, letting her see the bare truth: she was terrified for him. Terrified she'd fail. That if these sabotage runes resurfaced again, next time would be even worse. A surge that might prove fatal. Or unleash a wave of destruction that would turn the keep's walls into rubble.

She pressed her forehead to his shoulder. "You need to rest," she said, forcing calm into her tone even as her legs threatened to give out. "Let me check you in your chamber, see if we can re-anchor your wards,"

But Taron shook his head, shifting to press the faintest weight of his cheek against her hair. "Wait," he murmured. "Just...let me catch my breath. You, too."

Something in his voice, so raw with relief, made her chest tighten further. She drew a shaky inhale, inhaling the mix of soap, sweat, and scorched magic that clung to him. Outside, deeper in the corridor, panicked murmurs drifted. She sensed onlookers, guards or servants, hesitant to intrude but anxious to see if the crisis had passed.

Cassandra finally peeled her gaze away from him. Flames still smoldered in the ruined tapestry along the wall, forming a pocket of acrid smoke. A battered ornamental table was singed at the corners. She relinquished

Taron only enough to extend one hand, conjuring a small swirl of her own ward-light to snuff out the last of the embers. The faint glow illuminated Taron's face, letting her see how deeply the meltdown had exhausted him, shadows lingered under his eyes, though they still glinted with a subdued reflection of gratitude.

"It was sabotage," she said in a hushed voice for his ears alone. "Those runes we found near your chamber, they were either reactivated or we missed a second layer. I, I'm certain of it. This wasn't just your normal flux."

He let out a trembling breath, nodding in agreement. "I felt it earlier tonight, like something was tugging at my wards. But I didn't..." He paused to swallow. "I should've told you sooner, asked you to check thoroughly. I was worried about overburdening you. And then," He didn't finish, just shook his head heavily, shame flickering across his features.

She couldn't deny the spike of worry that flared in her gut. She pressed her hand lightly to his chest again, feeling his heart pound. "We'll figure out who's behind this," she vowed, forcing that old anger at the saboteurs into a steadier resolve. "But first, you need to sit. You're shaking."

He managed to make a wan smile, an expression that looked out of place on his drawn face. Gently, he allowed her to guide him deeper down the corridor, toward the open door of his chamber. The wards etched along the door frame flickered faintly, some partially marred by scorch marks. Cassandra felt a spike of renewed anger;

this was no accident. A saboteur had known precisely how to undermine Taron's carefully balanced aura.

Inside, the air was thick with residual energy, as though the meltdown had stained the entire space with an electric charge. A mirror lay shattered near the washbasin, and the shutters rattled in an unfelt breeze. She drew Taron toward the edge of his bed, where rumpled sheets bore fresh scorch marks at the corner. He sank onto the mattress with a hiss, burying his face in his hands.

She closed the door behind them, aware of the hush that followed. Likely, the guards posted themselves in the corridor to keep onlookers at bay. Her attention circled back to Taron. For a moment, she thought to fetch him water, or something to quell the leftover tremors in his aura, then realized her own legs were scarcely steady enough to cross the room.

"Let me see," she murmured, approaching him carefully. He lifted his head. She crouched in front of him, placing one hand on his thigh for balance and the other lightly atop his trembling left hand. "I want to do a final check for leftover flare-ups."

Taron nodded, letting her slip his hand free. She gently turned his arm palm up, scanning the faint runic cuff hugging his wrist. Thin lines glowed across the metal, a sign that it had suffered a near-overload. They would need to re-inscribe parts of it soon, or the next meltdown might slip beyond Cassandra's ability to contain.

Her chest tightened at the thought. Grimly, she rested her free hand over the cuff, letting a whisper of her power seep into its wards. A flicker of greenish light shimmered there, showing that at least the core engraving remained intact. Relief fluttered through her; catastrophic meltdown had been averted, but only barely.

"Taron," she said softly, not releasing his wrist. "If we were a minute slower, if another surge had hit,"

He exhaled, dropping his gaze. "I know."

She studied him in the flickering light of a single surviving candle still burning by the window. Beneath Taron's exhaustion loomed something else: shame. Perhaps at how reliant he was on her. Perhaps at the destruction left behind tonight. She watched the tension in his jaw and recognized the old guilt.

"Listen to me," she said, voice firm. "You didn't fail. Whoever planted these sabotage runes, they're the cause of this. You fought back. You survived. And I, I'm here because I choose to be, because I won't let them take you down."

A raw glimmer flickered in his eyes, and he swallowed, glancing away. "You say that, but everything around me ends up scorched," he said bitterly. "Every time I think I have a handle, something else chips away at my wards until they collapse. I'm so gods-damned bloody tired of it, Cassandra. Tired of feeling like a helpless,"

He cut himself off, but she felt the remainder of his words echo in his unsteady breath. Helpless child. Puppet prince. She understood that frustration too well. Gently, she laid a palm along the side of his face, forcing him to look at her. "Your power is part of who you are," she said, voice low. "Yes, it's dangerous, but you're fighting it every step of the way. Believe me, Taron, I see it."

He closed his eyes beneath her touch, leaning into her palm as though starving for comfort. The candle's glow cast flickering shadows across his features, accentuating the curve of his brow and the parted line of his lips. "You... should hate me," he murmured, the words trembling. "All that I let happen to you, my father's decree, yet you still stand with me."

Cassandra's mouth went dry. The old hurt lingered, as it always did, but it felt overshadowed in this moment by the fierce protectiveness that coursed through her. "I was furious," she admitted softly. "But I see how that guilt torments you. Let it go. We have enough enemies in this keep to fight, Taron." A shaky laugh escaped her. "We don't need to fight ourselves."

His eyes fluttered open, and for a heartbeat, neither spoke. She felt that thrumming awareness between them, familiar yet newly sharpened by the rawness of shared danger. The memory of holding him so close in the corridor, of siphoning his scorching magic, flared through her mind. Even now, the imprint of his body against hers lingered, reminding her how intense it was to cradle a power that could level a fortress, how intimate it felt to connect with him in that primal dance of wards and surges.

As though drawn by the same undertow, Taron's gaze flicked to her mouth. His breathing hitched. She could feel the tension in the air, a subtle, inevitable pull. Her heartbeat doubled, and for one dizzying moment, she thought they might tip forward, erase the last inch between them. The swirl of leftover magic in the room seemed to pulse around them, caught in the electric strand of unspoken longing.

Then Taron's hand slid up, fisting gently in her hair. The movement was tremulous but deliberate. He rested his forehead against hers, exhaling unsteadily. "Thank you," he said, voice ragged. "For saving me. Again."

CHAPTER

SIXTEEN

She closed her eyes. Deep in her chest, something ached at the husky texture of his gratitude. She wanted to brush aside that bone-deep guilt in him, to reassure him she wasn't leaving, that this sabotage would not break them. She wanted to stay in this hush a moment longer, suspended between heartbreak and something dangerously close to yearning.

Her lips parted to answer, but only a soft sound emerged, half an exhale, half a trembling sigh. With a ragged breath, Taron's fingers threaded more firmly through her hair, while his other hand steadied her shoulder. She felt the faint, labored pound of his heart echoing in her own chest. The swirl of leftover magic in the air might have been a thousand silent sparks, tugging them closer still.

The old wooden frame creaked under their combined weight. Her knee brushed his, and she felt a jolt of heat that was as much from Taron's aura as it was her own

112

quickening pulse. It worried her, how easily longing slipped in with tension and fear. She'd spent so long building walls against him, yet in these moments of raw desperation, they fell away.

She pressed a trembling hand over his chest, right where she felt the unsteady rhythm of his heart. "It's all right," she whispered. "No one else is here."

He nodded faintly, letting his eyes drift shut. And for the press of a single breath, they simply stayed like that, her palm against his heartbeat, his forehead tipped toward her hair, the hush broken only by the whisper of their breathing.

"I was scared," he admitted finally. "I thought, this time, maybe I wouldn't come back." His voice caught. "All I could see was that light, and it was tearing at me. Then I sensed you. You were...like a shield I could cling to."

Her throat constricted. "I felt you searching for me. And I'm not letting you go," she said, surprising herself with the quiet fierceness in her tone.

His eyes opened to meet her gaze, and for a lingering moment, they sought each other's expressions. She had no illusions that one rescue undid years of hurt, or that sabotage and betrayal were magically resolved. But in the hush of Taron's chamber, she glimpsed something else, a fragile but unwavering thread that bound them, forged through pain and necessity, yes, yet also through compassion and an unspoken need.

Around them, the room still bore signs of the meltdown: scorch marks on the curtains, fragments of the broken mirror, an uneasy static in the air. But Cassandra tuned out the chaos. Taron's voice lowered to a rasp, carrying a confession that hovered on his lips, too raw to ignore. She could see the shape of it in those parted lips, sense how months, no, years, of regret pressed behind every syllable.

She leaned closer, feeling the press of his breath against her cheek. Something in her chest fluttered, half fear, half longing. If he spoke that confession, if he uttered the words locked behind his guilt, she knew it would change everything. They were no longer exiled witch and desperate baron's heir, nor were they the naive friends of years past. They were two people who had sacrificed for each other in different ways, swallowing heartbreak and fear to keep themselves, or perhaps the entire barony, safe.

His grip on her hair slid downward, and his fingertips grazed her jaw. Even through the exhaustion, his touch trembled with a palpable current. She wondered if he felt that same coil inside, an aching swirl of closeness and heartbreak. The candlelight wavered, dancing across the ragged lines of worry on his face. She felt the unsteady pulse beneath her own skin, as if the meltdown's after-shocks lingered in them both.

A faint hush enfolded them, thick with possibility. She saw him swallow, breath hitching as he parted his lips to speak. "Cassandra, I," He broke off, brow furrowing. "When I, earlier tonight, I wanted to tell you,"

But before he could form the words, a fresh wave of dizziness seemed to grip him. His eyes fluttered, and his hand fell away from her jaw to clutch the edge of the mattress. Cassandra caught him around the shoulders, alarm shooting through her. She realized this particular meltdown had demanded far too much from him, he was battered, physically and magically.

"Ssh," she soothed, letting her free arm curl around his upper back, steadying him. "Don't push yourself. You're at your limit."

He gave a faint shake of his head, as though frustrated to be cut off. Then the tension drained from him, and he slumped forward into her embrace. A soft, knowing ache bloomed in her chest. Though part of her craved the words he'd nearly spoken, she recognized that he was on the verge of collapse. She adjusted her hold, guiding him carefully as his body sagged, letting his head come to rest against her shoulder.

For a moment, she simply held him, mindful of every tremor. The faint glow from the corridor seeped under the door, enough that she could see the lines of exhaustion marking his face. Carefully, gently, she traced her hand along the base of his neck, channeling a gentle healing hum that would soothe frayed nerves and calm the echoes of his surge.

His breath hitched again, yet this time it was a softer, less frantic sound. She could feel tension easing from his muscles, a surrender to blessed relief after so many minutes of raw struggle. Her own exhaustion throbbed, but she ignored it, focusing all her attention on him.

The hush lingered until Taron, in a low voice close to her ear, whispered, "Don't leave yet." It wasn't a commanding tone, only a broken plea.

She smoothed a damp lock of hair back from his forehead, her fingers lingering far too gently for someone who once swore she'd keep a wall between them. But that wall was so fractured now. "I won't," she said, sealing it with the quiet conviction that he needed to hear.

Slowly, his breath found a measured pace. His eyelids drooped, half-lidded, as though dragging him under. Cassandra felt her own limbs grow heavy in response, the draining aftermath of channeling so much magic. She discovered that she, too, was trembling from head to toe. Yet despite the fatigue, she was acutely aware of how intimately they were pressed together, her thighs brushed his, the side of her hip against his waist, his fingers still entangled in the ends of her hair.

If someone entered right now, they would see a scandalous sight: the baron's heir slumped in the arms of the exiled witch. But Cassandra couldn't find the will to care. Something told her that Taron, either, was long past worrying what people might whisper. In this moment, safety was all that mattered.

His chest rose in another shaky breath. One of his hands, still trembling, slid up to curl over her shoulder, then to her neck. She stayed still, letting him explore that tentative contact. His fingertips brushed the side of her throat, so faint that she shivered at the warm, careful pressure. A question lurked in his expression, as though he worried she might flinch away.

She didn't. Instead, she found herself leaning into the touch, heart speeding. Her free hand clutched at the front of his torn tunic, just enough to keep them close. In the candle's soft glow, Taron's eyes, though half-lidded, shone with an emotion she recognized from old memories of quiet nights in the orchard, stolen glances they once shared before everything fell apart. Longing, regret, devotion, all knotted together in the corners of his gaze.

His grip moved higher, tangling in her hair near the nape of her neck. A shaky exhale parted his lips; she felt it against her temple. And then, in a near-silent murmur, he said her name again, cradling each syllable as though it were precious.

Cassandra's heart twisted. She pressed her forehead lightly to his, eyes drifting shut. The keep was silent around them, as if the entire fortress held its breath, waiting for the next moment. Seconds stretched as they sat there, bodies entwined at the edge of his bed. Her exhaustion warred with the molten swirl of feelings bursting inside her chest. She thought of the sabotage that tried to tear his wards apart, the vile runes that nearly destroyed him tonight. But those saboteurs had miscalculated one crucial factor: she would never let Taron face them alone.

At last, the tension bled out of Taron's posture. His shoulders slumped in true surrender, letting the enormity of fatigue claim him. Turning his face into the curve of her neck, he breathed, "Cassandra...please stay," as though those words were the only tether he had left.

She bowed her head, letting the weight of his hair slip through her fingers. Gently, she eased him down so he could rest, keeping her arms around him to stave off the chill that so often followed a meltdown. His legs shifted on the mattress, boots scraping the floor. For a moment, they both halfway reclined, propped on the bed's edge.

Bright afterimages still danced behind her eyelids from the corridor's earlier flare of magic. The memory of Taron's surging aura burned in her mind. She remembered the scorching arcs of light that threatened to split him apart, the surge that hammered the corridor's walls, the near-fatal tension of guiding that molten energy through her wards. This time, they succeeded. Next time?

No. She couldn't let her thoughts stray further. Right now, he was safe, and that was victory enough.

Taron, near the boundary of consciousness, gave one final, shuddering sigh. Then his fingers, still curled in her hair, slid through the strands in a halting caress, as though he could scarcely believe she was tangible and real. She felt the careful pressure of his fingertips brush her scalp, sending a ripple of sensation down her back. Heat fluttered in her chest, blending with a protective ache she could hardly name. In the hush, her heart pounded, so loud in her ears that it nearly drowned out everything else.

She realized with dizzy certainty that they had crossed a threshold tonight. This was no longer about grudging alliances or old resentments. Something deeper had taken root in the quiet space between them, in the press of their bodies and the aftershocks of shared crisis. He was all she had to quell the barony's panic. She was all he had to stop the meltdown from consuming him. Their fates were irrevocably wound together, had been since the day she'd first discovered her talent to anchor his dangerous magic, and as it turned out, anchor his soul as well.

Her breath caught at the thought. "Taron," she whispered, glancing down at the exhausted line of his face. Embers of desire warred with the gravity of their predicament. For now, though, she soothed her fingertips across his temple, feeling him settle into her touch with a soft exhale. She brushed aside a damp strand of hair. "Sleep, if you can. I'm here."

He mustered a faint, grateful sound. His hand finally stilled in her hair, sliding to curl around her shoulder in a loose hold. The weight of his head pressed gently against her collarbone, offering more intimacy than all the formal gestures in the world. She felt her cheeks grow hot, but she didn't shift away. Let the keep whisper if they must. She would not leave him to fend off nightmares alone.

Together, they breathed. Her senses caught a faint trace of smoke lingering in the air, the mellow glow of the solitary candle, the hush of the corridor beyond, where guards likely hovered, waiting for any sign of fresh disaster. But inside this chamber, a fragile peace had settled, forged from desperation and sealed by that final, exhausted embrace.

Cassandra closed her eyes, exhaustion tugging at every limb, but not quite willing to let herself sleep. She grasped Taron's hand, interlacing their fingers carefully over the charred bedcover. His pulse felt steady, though faint. She had done her duty, yes, but more than that, she had saved the person whose presence had once broken her heart. And in the dark corners of her mind, she understood with startling clarity that Taron was the only one who could truly understand the tangled darkness she carried from exile and betrayal. Together, in moments like this, it was as though the rest of the world and its accusations ceased to matter.

His breathing deepened; each inhalation less ragged than the last. A faint murmur escaped him, some heartfelt word she couldn't make out, but she guessed it was for her. She couldn't stop the tiny, sorrow-tinged smile that tugged at her lips. Let him rest, she thought, smoothing her palm down his back once more. Tomorrow's problems, Baron Ulric's skepticism, the rival saboteur's next move, would wait. Tonight, they had this small victory, and one another.

BRIGHT AFTER-IMAGES from the corridor's surge still danced in her mind's eye, searing memories of almost losing Taron to a sabotage-laced meltdown. But night's quiet calm had returned, rocking them gently in exhaustion's arms. She felt Taron's body go slack with the release of tension. The candle's flame guttered but held, casting a thin wavering glow across their tangled forms.

When Taron finally stirred once more, his fingers drifting through her hair in that soft, wonderstruck motion, she bit her lip at the rush of emotion that struck her. Their closeness, the lingering press of his breath against her collarbone, everything felt magnified in the hush. A faint flush curled through her abdomen, part protective, part longing, all inescapable. This was not merely relief or sympathy; it was the raw pulse of tethered hearts acknowledging how deeply they needed each other.

Her eyes stung with tears she refused to let fall. Instead, she bent her head, pressing a feather-light kiss to his temple, letting her lips linger on the damp skin as she inhaled the faint tang of leftover magic. She felt him exhaling against her collarbone, the quiet trembling of someone on the brink of words he was too shattered to say.

And in that moment, Cassandra knew that everything had changed. The distance once carved by betrayal was no longer insurmountable. It was simply overshadowed by the realization that together, they formed something stronger, an unspoken promise that neither sabotage nor baronial threats could erase. He was all she had to keep the barony from plunging into ruin, and she was all that kept him from tearing himself apart. If that truth carried them to danger, so be it. She would face it for him, and with him.

Drained beyond measure, Taron finally slipped into a light doze, his fingers still loosely entwined in her hair. Cassandra cradled him in the glow of the guttering candle, feeling each slow, steady breath as the quiet minutes passed. Her arms ached, her wards felt spent, but she remained vigil. In that hush, one more moment stretched, beating in time with the tender, unspoken claim that crackled between them, fragile yet unbreakable.

Outside, the corridor settled into silence, albeit one that hovered at the edge of disaster. But for now, Taron was safe in her arms, and that was the only victory that mattered. She would watch over him until dawn if necessary. Because amid the swirling sabotage and all the heartbreak that had once parted them, she realized that Taron's very life, and perhaps her own hope, depended on this fierce, unbreakable bond.

His warm breath against her skin was the last sensation she let herself register. The final remnants of the meltdown flickered behind her eyelids like echoes of distant lightning, whispering that tomorrow would bring fresh trials. But tonight, her vigil was here in Taron's chamber, holding him until sunlit morning. Eventually, her own exhaustion weighed too heavy; she drifted into a restless half-sleep, still upright, still cradling him.

In that half-waking quiet, Taron stirred again, just barely, and shifted against her, letting his fingers slip through her hair one final time in wordless gratitude. A soft sound, almost a sigh, escaped his lips, brushing warmth across her collarbone. Despite the layers of conflict still waiting outside this room, Cassandra felt her heart clench at his gentle, unguarded touch.

Yes, she thought hazily, her cheeks were hot even in the dimness, they were all each other had. And for now, that tether was enough to keep the world from shattering beneath them both.

CHAPTER

SEVENTEEN

Cassandra jerked awake to the sound of pounding at her chamber door. Dawn's faint light filtered past her shuttered window, and her heart lurched with a surge of unease. She heard muffled voices, urgent, agitated. For a moment, the warmth lingering in her bed held her captive; her eyelids felt heavy from a near-sleepless night in Taron's quarters. But the frantic knocks continued, and a sharp edge of dread pushed her upright.

She stood, threw on a warmer cloak, and rasped out, "Yes, I'm coming!" The hinges creaked as she opened the door. Sir Barro and another knight, breathless, loomed outside. Sir Barro's expression was graver than she'd ever seen.

"Farmland's been attacked," he said without preamble. "Whole sections scorched, or so the messengers claim."

Cassandra's stomach dropped. A low hum of tension gathered behind her eyes. "Scorched?"

The older knight just behind Barro cleared his throat. "Villagers came at first light, demanding help. Seems it's Taron's power done it, but we don't know how or why."

A flicker of anger rose in Cassandra's chest, though she kept her voice even. "Then we'll find out. Let me gather my things."

She snatched up her belt pouch, fumbling a little as she fit her folded chalk inside. The last time Taron's magic rampaged; the keep's corridors had nearly gone up in flames. If the farmland was marked with scorch lines, it might be sabotage again, someone tampering with the outer wards that linked to Taron's aura. The implications made her skin prickle with dread. If the saboteurs discovered how to provoke Taron across such a distance, they now possessed a far more dangerous weapon.

Sir Barro, the knight escorted her downstairs, boots echoing on stone as they converged in the keep's court-yard. There, Taron paced restlessly, arms crossed over his chest. Even in the bleary dawn, she caught the flicker of raw magic around him. The faint blue-white sheen pulsed over his hands; half cloaked by his dark riding gloves. She gritted her teeth at the sight, the signs of his powers being on edge, threatening to surge again.

His gaze snapped up to hers, worry etched into every line of his face. "They're saying the farmland," he began, voice taut. "I, I didn't intentionally,"

"We'll figure it out," she cut in softly. Words tumbled unbidden: You wouldn't do that. You would never just burn farmland. But she didn't voice them aloud. Ever since the last sabotage, she'd known better than to assume any shred of logic would quell people's fear.

Already, two stable hands wrestled with the horses, trying to fit saddles and bridles in frantic haste, while a handful of knights readied themselves for the ride out. In the corner of the courtyard, she caught a glimpse of Baron Ulric's tall silhouette. He was barking orders at a steward, the baron's hair bristling under the meager sunrise. Tension coiled in her stomach. Despite her standoff against him in the council chamber days ago, he remained the official authority. And if farmland was damaged, he would not hesitate to blame Taron, or more precisely, Cassandra, for failing to rein in Taron's magic.

A stablehand approached with a dappled mare for Cassandra. She murmured thanks and swung astride, ignoring the way her pulse rattled. Taron mounted his black gelding, shoulders stiff. Sir Barro rode forward, hand raised in a sign to move. They trotted out through the keep's great gates and onto the open roads that led into farmland. Horses' hooves thundered on hardened dirt, stirring up the crisp morning air.

Cassandra's cloak snapped behind her as they picked up pace. Half a dozen knights accompanied them, exchanging uneasy looks whenever Taron's horse drew too near. The unspoken fear was obvious: If Taron's aura flared mid-ride, even the fastest knight might be singed. She swallowed down frustration. He was trying, fighting so hard to keep it contained. She knew better than anyone how sensitive Taron's wards had become. Any tampering at the farmland warding posts could sever the delicate balance she'd re-anchored around him. And if that balance was gone...

"Are you all right?" she shouted over the galloping din, twisting to look at Taron.

He inclined his head, jaw set. "Yes, but," He hesitated, scanning the rolling fields up ahead. "I can feel something. A pull. Like my aura is...reaching out." Fear ghosted across his eyes. "It feels wrong."

Her chest clenched. Time was short, then. She urged her mare forward, ignoring the chill that trickled down her spine. Half the farmland was still concealed by early-morning haze. Smoke, or perhaps low mist, blurred the horizon. Yet as they rode closer, an acrid smell threaded through the air, like burned tinder and charred leaves. Cassandra's stomach twisted. She knew that smell well from nights spent containing Taron's surges.

It took nearly half an hour of hard riding before the farmland's devastation came into view. The fields here were wide and open, scattered with half-grown winter crops. In the distance, orchard trees rose in neat rows. But the west fields, the ones nearest the bank of the slow-moving river, lay in blackened ruins. Smoke still curled from the scorched earth, and a few villagers huddled by the fences, wide-eyed with shock. At the sight of Taron and the knights, they recoiled.

Taron swallowed, sliding off his horse. Cassandra dismounted as well, though more slowly, dread lodging in her throat. She set her mare's reins aside and picked her way across the ashen ground. Just a day ago, this land likely teemed with green shoots. Now, dark streaks marred the soil, as though a massive wave of fire had swept across in a single pass.

"By the spirits," Sir Barro muttered, turning in a slow circle. "It's...like the orchard corridor all over again, only bigger."

A strangled feeling welled in Cassandra's chest. She crouched, brushing her fingertips across the blackened ground. Still warm. Little puffs of soot rose beneath her touch, and she sensed the faint residue of Taron's magical signature, like a ghostly echo humming along her own wards. Anger flared within her, mingled with an edge of panic. Someone had manipulated Taron's aura so that it manifested here.

"Cassandra," Taron said hoarsely, coming up behind her. "You feel it too, don't you?"

She nodded, glancing over her shoulder. "This is your magic. But I know you didn't do it deliberately." She cast her gaze around. "The question is how."

A hushed, upset murmur rippled among the knights. Two villagers who'd approached from the fence line began muttering under their breath, something about "witch's wards failing us." Cassandra tried not to stiffen at the pointed emphasis on witch. Instead, she rose to her feet, ignoring the flush of resentment warming her cheeks.

She glimpsed movement in the corner of her eye, Baron Ulric's retinue arriving. He rode up astride a tall bay horse, slicing through the group of stunned knights, his brow a thundercloud of resentment. In a long stride, he dismounted, landing heavily in the ash-laden field. A swirl of tension followed him, as though he carried authority like a sword.

He wasted no time. "What is the meaning of this?" he demanded, gaze flicking accusingly from Taron to Cassandra. "Another meltdown?" The baron's voice rang with contempt. "You'd best have answers, witch."

Cassandra's grip whitened around the handful of sooty grass she still held. Anger threatened to ripple through her, but she forced calm. "I only just arrived, my lord. I intend to investigate whether someone tampered with Taron's wards at the farmland posts. Same as they've done inside the keep."

A snort. "Sabotage, always sabotage," he said, voice dripping with disbelief. "If you had anchored Taron properly, these farmland wards wouldn't have cracked."

She forced herself to remain steady, even as her heart drummed with anger. "My wards cannot hold if they're being deliberately unraveled. We've seen evidence of sabotage in the keep. Now, it seems the saboteur has extended it here, as far as Taron's aura can reach."

Ulric's lip curled. "Convenient excuse but look around you." He gestured at the scorched soil with disgust. "I see evidence only that Taron's magic has flared and ruined these fields. The question is who allowed it to happen."

Before Cassandra could retort, another stir of noise erupted behind them. Two knights cried out, "Taron!" She spun around in time to see Taron clasping one hand to his temple, doubling over as if in pain. A pulse of silver-blue light danced across his form in a crackling shimmer. She recognized it with a flash of horror: an oncoming surge.

EIGHTEEN

"Taron," She lurched toward him.

He staggered, shoulders jerking, as if an invisible tide inside him strained to breach all barriers. Magic arced at his fingertips. A handful of knights instinctively drew back, hands flying to their sword hilts. Sir Barro hesitated only a moment before stepping forward, as though to support Taron physically.

"Stay away!" Taron gasped; voice hoarse. "I can't control it,"

Too late. A burst of shimmering energy snapped outward. Sir Barro ducked with a grunt, narrowly avoiding a lash of raw magic. Another knight who was too close yelped as sparks seared his cloak. He stumbled to the ground, rolling away in panic. Cassandra's heart hammered, and she sprinted forward, fumbling for a piece of warding chalk in her pouch. She had mere seconds before Taron lost the fragile tether to rationality.

"Hold on," she whispered, more a command to herself

than to Taron. She reached him, ignoring how arcs of energy hissed against her own wards. Her fingers brushed his elbow. The sensation was of scorching heat just beneath the fabric of his coat. He jerked away, pained, but she caught hold of his wrist and flung up a quick focusing rune with her free hand.

The air crackled, saturated with Taron's aura. Cassandra's vision blurred, but she forced her eyes open. She poured the smallest thread of her magic into his wards, attempting to anchor him, bracing for the staggering shock of his surge. If she could ground it, just a fraction, maybe they could avoid more devastation.

Her chalk-laced fingertips traced a swift pattern across the back of Taron's glove. "Steady," she murmured. "Stay with me."

Sweat beaded along Taron's brow. For a terrifying instant, the swirl of raw magic redoubled, nearly knocking her breath from her lungs. She heard the anxious shouts of knights scattering, presumably to avoid being singed. Another wave pulsed outward. Sir Barro, crouched nearby, shielded his face as sparks bit the air. In the distance, she thought she heard Baron Ulric calling Taron's name, but the baron's voice was almost lost beneath the roar of uncontained energy.

Hands shaking, Cassandra pressed her palm to the faintly glowing runes on Taron's cuff. She willed her own magic to feed it, reasserting the containment weave she'd painstakingly built. "Let it flow through me," she whispered. "Don't fight alone."

Taron's eyes flickered open, wild with fear. But

beneath it, she sensed that he recognized her voice. He grit his teeth, clinging to her presence. Another shudder wracked him, but the sparks slowed, losing some of their chaotic force. Cassandra exhaled in a trembling wave of relief, coaxing the last of the surge into a controlled funnel. Slowly, painfully, she channeled the worst of his magic into the ground. A crackle of light raced along the scorched earth, dissipating into the soil with a soft sizzle.

When at last the air fell still, Taron sagged in her grasp. Cassandra's lungs burned from the exertion, but she forced a steady breath, winding her arms around his torso to keep them both upright. His chest rose and fell in shallow, shuddering motions.

For a moment, no one moved. The knights stood in a tense ring, blades half-drawn, as if uncertain the threat had truly passed. Sir Barro, a gash on his cheek from flying embers, rose with a grimace. He took a cautious step forward. At Cassandra's slight nod, he relaxed. Taron's aura no longer flared with the threat of immediate meltdown.

"This is what we've come to?" The Baron advanced, ignoring the ashen soil swirling around his boots. "We ride here to investigate farmland destruction, and Taron nearly incinerates my knights in the process?" He shot Cassandra a blistering look. "Your wards are failing, witch."

Cassandra pulled herself straighter, though she still clutched Taron's trembling form. "My wards are being tampered with," she said, forcing an even tone. "Can't you see? This was triggered by sabotage. Taron can't control his magic if someone else is fighting against him."

She glanced at Taron's face, anguished lines etched around his eyes. He drew in a ragged breath, as if trying to muster words, but he only managed to say, "Father, I, I didn't... She's helping."

Ulric latched on to Taron's uncertain posture, advancing until his shadow fell across them both. "Yes, she's helping," he echoed with bitter sarcasm. "And look at the results." He waved a dismissive hand at the scorched fields around them. "You think the peasants will feel safe? They already fear Taron's magic. Now, they see him nearly unleashing it on his own men." His gaze bored into Cassandra. "They see you doing nothing to prevent it."

Fury coiled within Cassandra's chest. "I contained him," she said evenly, "not that you'll acknowledge it. If I hadn't intervened, Taron's surge might have been far worse."

Several anxious knights stirred at that, quietly acknowledging the truth. But she saw a handful of suspicious nobles, arrived with Ulric's retinue, exchanging pointed, disapproving looks. One of them, a tall, hawkish man wearing a half-cape, stepped forward.

"That's all supposition," the noble said. "From our vantage, it appears Taron's meltdown continues to grow more frequent. Clearly, the wards aren't working. Perhaps they're even fueling this chaos." His gaze slid over Cassandra. "Forgive me, my lord, but if the saboteur is never found, might it be because we're looking at the wrong person?"

Cassandra's stomach clenched, and an angry flush rose up her neck. Wicked rumors had circulated in the keep of late, hinting she was behind Taron's surges. Now, out here in the farmland, that same poisonous suspicion was rearing its head again. She felt Taron tense at her side, as though he longed to speak. But the baron's presence weighed heavily.

Ulric said nothing, his silence damning. Then he turned toward the ring of knights. "Secure the area," he barked. "Let no one tamper with the farmland posts before Cassandra demonstrates her so-called sabotage theory." Sarcasm laced his final words. "If it exists, perhaps she'll be good enough to show proof this time."

Cassandra's pulse thrummed with frustration. Proof, like the half-scraped sabotage runes she had found in Taron's corridor days ago, or the suspicious footprints, or the forged ledgers with her name. But none of it had satisfied Ulric. She inhaled until her lungs ached.

Sir Barro cleared his throat. "We might want to check the nearest warding post first, my lord." He gestured toward a weathered wooden stake standing at the far edge of the blackened field. "It's carved with runes meant to tie into Lord Taron's aura."

Ulric gave a curt nod. "Do so. All of you. Let's see if the sabotage is real or just another excuse."

As knights spread out, Cassandra helped Taron straighten. She kept her voice low, mindful of the curious watchers. "Are you all right?"

He nodded shakily, meeting her gaze. In that fleeting exchange, she felt his guilt like a physical weight pressing against her. She recognized the swirl of shame for nearly harming Sir Barro and the simmer of frustration that he couldn't seem to shield Cassandra from blame. He parted his lips, as if to apologize, but couldn't quite form words.

She squeezed his arm gently. "Let's focus," she said. "We need to see if the farmland posts mirror the tampering in the keep."

He swallowed. "Yes," he murmured thickly. Then, with halting steps, they headed toward the nearest post, stepping carefully around lumps of ashen grass and the occasional smoking tuft. Sir Barro and a cluster of knights trailed closer, watchful but not interfering.

The wooden post rose about chest-high, set in the ground with thick iron brackets. Its surface was etched with runes that glowed faintly in bright daylight, an unnerving sign, since farmland wards typically shone only under direct magical usage. Cassandra knelt beside it, ignoring the ash that stained her knees. Careful not to disturb anything, she ran her fingertips over the wood, seeking scratched lines or mismatched symbols.

"Taron, look here," she murmured, pointing to a swirl of runes near the post's base. "There's a layering effect... like someone carved fresh lines over the older wards." As she leaned in, her breath caught. "This curvature is identical to the sabotage runes we found in the orchard corridor."

Sir Barro stooped beside her. "So, it's the same saboteur," he concluded grimly. "And the pattern...could it force Taron's aura to flare outward?"

Cassandra nodded. "Yes. These farmland posts are magically linked to Taron. They're designed to ground his aura when it spikes, distributing minor bursts of energy safely into the earth, so the farmland draws strength from him in a controlled way. But if someone inverted the runes, the posts would draw out Taron's power forcibly, destabilizing him instead."

Behind her, Taron let out a slow exhale. She glanced up to see him staring at the charred rings of soil around them. "That's why I felt like something was yanking at me," he rasped, pressing a hand to his temple. "No wonder I lost control."

Ulric's voice cut in, sharp as a blade. "And yet," he said, stepping forward with folded arms, "we only have your word that these runes are sabotage." He gestured for one of his personal aides to step up. "Bring me a mage scribe. I want a second opinion on whether these runes are genuinely new, or if Cassandra is conjuring illusions."

Cassandra bristled. "You can have your entire keep examine it, my lord. The proof is here." She traced a fine circle around the suspicious lines. "Notice the grooves, fresher wood. The weathered surface is worn smooth, but these cuts are sharper, not eroded. This is all new." A soft, bitter laugh escaped her. "If you want to question illusions, read the grain of the wood. It's not that easy to fake."

Several knights hunkered closer, peering at the post. Perhaps even they could see the difference between old, faded runes and new, freshly carved ones. Cassandra's heart pounded, adrenaline surging from both anger and relief that she might finally have tangible evidence.

One of the suspicious nobles stepped back with a scoff. "This proves nothing," he muttered. "For all we know, Cassandra sneaked out last night, carved these lines herself, and then used her wards to orchestrate this meltdown, so she could point fingers. She was exiled for a reason."

The words hung in the sooty air, twisting Cassandra's stomach. Cold fury churned inside her, but she forced her chin up, refusing to break her composure. She sensed Taron tense behind her, as though he yearned to snap back. A glance at his tightly pressed lips told her he was wrestling with the ingrained fear of contradicting these nobles, and the guilt that he'd once stood silent while she was exiled. The memory must sting, especially now, when people hurled the same hateful accusations.

She pushed to her feet, turning to face the man who'd spoken. "I was exiled on falsified pretenses," she said calmly. "I've fought to protect Taron's aura every day since I returned. Anyone with eyes can see I just contained his surge. I'd be a fool to cause the meltdown I risk my life to prevent."

Some villagers at the periphery murmured, uncertain. She could sense their confusion. On one hand, Taron's meltdown had scorched their fields. On the other hand, Cassandra was the only one stepping forward to unravel its cause. Tension crackled in the very air.

Ulric held up a hand, silencing the rabble. Then he

pinned Cassandra with a look full of cold calculation. "You claim sabotage is certain," he said. "But sabotage or not, the farmland is ruined. My knights were nearly incinerated by Taron's outburst." His gaze darted to Taron, a flicker of disappointment in his eyes. "We cannot ignore the fact that your wards failed to stop this before it began."

Cassandra's throat constricted. "I can't stop sabotage if it's not investigated thoroughly," she hissed. "You dismissed every piece of evidence I brought you."

He drew himself up, arms clasped behind his back, and his expression was stony. "Let me be plain: if you can't prevent Taron's surges, you are of no use. The farmland has lost a crucial field. My people are terrified." He paused, letting the hush deepen. "You have one purpose here, Cassandra: to keep Taron's aura in check. If you cannot, then perhaps we should consider alternative arrangements."

NINETEEN

nger and hurt battered her. She recalled all the times she'd stabilized Taron, saved the orchard from burning, saved the keep from exploding into chaos. Now she stood on scorched farmland, savage proof that sabotage had escalated, and the baron hurled blame at her feet. As if the saboteur's cunning was her personal failing. A tremor of rage lit her limbs, but she forced her fists to remain at her sides.

Taron's voice, raw and hoarse, cut through the silence. "Father," he said, "stop this. Cassandra is right, someone's tampering with the wards. You know she's not at fault. If she were, she wouldn't have saved me just now." A swirl of frustration underpinned his tone. "I'm telling you; we faced sabotage within the keep. Sir Barro has seen the evidence. It's the same pattern here."

All eyes pivoted to Sir Barro. He cleared his throat, nodding slowly. "I...have indeed witnessed runes that do not match Cassandra's style. Every time we find them;

they point to a culprit forging her name." He looked at the baron, uneasy. "My lord, the orchard fiasco had identical sabotage."

Ulric's grim expression betrayed a flicker of vexation, as though he disliked hearing a knight corroborating her story. Still, he said stiffly, "If that is so, we shall intensify the search for these alleged forgeries." His glance slid back to Cassandra. "But know this: the suspicion in my court grows daily. I can't silence the chatter that you manipulate Taron to your advantage. If your wards were truly strong, no saboteur would so easily unravel them."

"That's not how magic works," she snapped, voice shaking with suppressed fury. "Wards can be disrupted by cunning infiltration. If you refuse to coordinate an official inquiry, you're giving the culprit free rein." Her voice rose without meaning to. "We need to isolate the forging of runic materials, question the supply logs, cross-check every last scribble,"

"You do not dictate how I run my barony," he snarled.

Cassandra bit her tongue so hard the taste of blood pricked it. This was hopeless. The farmland was charred, Taron's meltdown was fresh in every mind, and the baron was determined to cast blame. Meanwhile, a handful of suspicious nobles took in the sight of her and Taron standing together like lightning rods, fueling their own narratives about witches and uncontained magic.

She breathed in, forcing calm. That was when Taron's hand brushed hers. A light, desperate contact, easily missed by onlookers. She felt the tremor in his fingers, the raw undercurrent of his remorse. "Cassandra," he said under his breath, so softly no one else could hear, "I'm sorry."

Her chest constricted. She curled her own fingertips around his for a single trembling heartbeat. She knew his apology was layered, sorry for failing to protect the farmland, sorry for nearly hurting Sir Barro, sorry for not confronting his father more forcefully, sorry for not stopping the rumors. It spun an aching web in her chest. Their gazes locked for a moment, intense and burdened with all the words they couldn't speak under so many watchful stares.

Then she gently eased her hand away, remembering the circle of knights, the villagers staring, the baron's disapproving presence. She stepped toward the blackened post again, voice shifting to a brisk, controlled tone. "We've identified sabotage runes on this post. I'd wager the others dotted around these fields are similarly marred." She turned to a few knights. "Would you check them, please? If we see the same pattern repeated, it cements the sabotage theory."

Sir Barro dipped his head and motioned for two men to accompany him. They wove through the farmland, heading toward the other warding posts that ringed the property. Across the field, half-burned fences and scattered lumps of dirt made the going treacherous, but Cassandra suspected they would find more signs of tampering. The saboteur had systematically weakened Taron's entire ward network. Fury flared again. How many times would these hidden enemies push Taron to the brink?

Baron Ulric regarded her with a narrowed gaze. "If your search reveals matching runes, we'll consider the possibility that sabotage is real. But bear in mind, Cassandra, if this fails to produce conclusive evidence," He let the threat trail off, heavy with implication.

"I understand," she said in a low voice.

Taron glowered at his father. "You act as though you want her to fail," he said, voice tight, though he reined in open defiance. "She's saved me more times than I can count. Doesn't that count for anything?"

Ulric's lip twitched. "It doesn't matter if she lets the farmland go up in flames."

Those words stung like a slap, intensifying the tension around them. Cassandra pressed her lips together, choosing silence. She could not afford a shouting match, not here, not when the frightened villagers and knights looked on. Instead, she pivoted discreetly to look at the ring of onlookers. Some watchers wore sorrowful expressions, others still burned with suspicion. The mention of farmland up in flames at Taron's hand was bound to echo across the region, fueling more rumors. The festival orchard had recovered from the last surge, but farmland was the barony's lifeblood. If peasants believed Taron was behind it, believed Cassandra's wards were, indeed, suspect and she would be accused of being complicit. Any fragile trust she'd earned might vanish.

Taron's anger flared like the surge they'd just contained. He stepped forward, his shoulders squared, and the weight of his presence silenced the murmurs in the crowd. His voice cut through the tension, sharp and forceful. "Enough, Father."

The baron turned to him with a glare, but Taron didn't flinch. He took another step, closing the distance between them. The air around him seemed to hum with restrained energy, the faint glimmer of his magic visible in the charged atmosphere. "You keep talking about the farmland, about the fear of your people, but you're blind to what's right in front of you. Cassandra saved me. Again. She's the only reason this entire field isn't still burning."

Ulric's lip curled, but Taron pressed on, his voice rising with barely contained fury. "You act as though sabotaged wards are some convenient excuse, but it's not a theory—it's a fact. Barro has seen the forged runes. I've seen them. Yet you dismiss it, as though it's easier to blame Cassandra than to confront the truth.

Ulric narrowed his eyes. "Do not presume to tell me how to run my barony, Taron. I am trying to protect our people—"

"No," Taron interrupted, his tone hard and unyielding. "You're trying to protect your pride. You can't stand the idea that you might have missed the danger, that someone under your nose has been working against us. So instead, you blame the one person who's been fighting to fix it."

The tension in the crowd was palpable, but Taron didn't stop. He turned, gesturing toward the scorched land around them. "Do you think I don't know what people are saying? That I'm a danger, a liability? That Cassandra's the cause of it all?" He faced his father again, his jaw tight. "But you know better. You know she's done nothing but keep me alive, keep this barony standing, and still, you undermine her at every turn."

Ulric opened his mouth, but Taron's magic flared, a sharp crackle of energy that made the air ripple. It wasn't wild or destructive—Taron held it in check with a precision that spoke volumes. Even Cassandra felt her breath catch, the controlled intensity of his power unlike anything she'd seen before.

"I won't let you treat her like this," Taron said, his voice quieter now but no less resolute. "You want someone to blame for the farmland? Blame me. Blame the sabotage. But don't you dare put this on Cassandra. She deserves better than that, and you know it."

The baron's expression faltered for a moment, a flicker of surprise crossing his face as he regarded his son. The raw defiance, the unwavering conviction—it wasn't the first time Taron had stood up to him, but there was something different now. Something final.

Taron's gaze swept the gathered crowd, his voice carrying across the field. "You all saw what happened today. You saw her save me. You saw the runes she uncovered. If anyone doubts her dedication, if anyone thinks she's the cause of this, speak now."

The murmurs began again, but they were different this time—less suspicious, more uncertain. Sir Barro, standing off to the side, gave a slow nod of approval, and a few knights exchanged glances before stepping forward to inspect the posts Cassandra had pointed out.

Ulric's voice, when it finally came, was quieter but no less cold. "You've made your point, Taron. But don't mistake my patience for weakness. If this investigation yields no proof of sabotage, the consequences will be severe."

Taron didn't move, his magic still humming faintly in the air. "Then I'll find the proof myself," he said firmly. "And I'll make sure everyone knows who's really to blame."

CHAPTER

TWENTY

Gradually, the morning light brightened, casting harsh clarity over the blackened swaths of ground. The smell of smoke clung to everything. A farmwife approached the baron, face taut with desperation, mumbling about the loss of next season's harvest. The baron nodded gravely, patting her shoulder with rehearsed concern. Cassandra felt a twist of guilt. She wished she could comfort the villagers, but they looked at her like an omen. Instead, she crouched by Taron again, watching the swirl of magic still faintly trembling at his fingertips.

"Does it still hurt?" she asked softly, trying not to draw the baron's attention again.

He flexed his hand. "It's more numbness now. Like something was ripping out part of me." A frustrated exhale parted his lips. Then, lower still: "Cassandra, I wish,"

He didn't finish. She saw in his eyes a stricken swirl of

regret, regret that they'd come to this point, that he'd ever let her be exiled, that he still couldn't fully stand between her and his father's rage. She offered him a trembling half-smile. She, too, wished for so many things undone. But no words could fix the charred soil at their feet.

Just then, Sir Barro returned, flanked by two uncomfortable knights. Their expressions confirmed Cassandra's suspicions. Barro's stern face was grimmer than ever. "Every post is tampered with," he announced. "Carvings that differ from the original ward structure. The sabotage is consistent across all of them."

That admission stirred a fresh wave of murmurs. A flicker of triumph sparked in Cassandra's chest, finally, solid proof. She reached to rest a hand on Taron's shoulder, a subtle sign of reassurance.

Ulric's expression was difficult to read. Under normal circumstances, the baron might be forced to concede that Cassandra had been correct about sabotage. But she saw the calculation warring behind his eyes. Admitting sabotage also meant admitting he had to take real measures to uncover the culprit, measures that might disrupt the barony's comfortable routines. Worse, from his perspective, it might give Cassandra credibility he did not want her to have.

He flicked his gaze to the suspicious noble in the half-cape. "Send word to the keep," he said. "We'll dispatch scribes and guards to dismantle these new runes. Ensure no one touches them until the scribes arrive." He paused, glacial. "As for you, Cassandra, you will remain under watch until this is resolved. I won't have you interfering with the evidence."

Frustration sizzled along her nerves. "Fine," she bit out, "but we should remove these sabotage runes carefully. The farmland can't afford another surge."

Ulric's mouth pinched into a thin line. "We will see that it's handled. You, however, will step back. For all we know, your meddling might compound the problem."

Taron's eyes flared with protest, but Cassandra placed a cautionary hand on his arm. She knew better than to argue in circles. Instead, she nodded once, turning away from the baron to direct her attention to Sir Barro. "Until your scribes come, these wards remain active. If Taron strays too close, they could provoke another meltdown. Keep him at a distance."

Sir Barro dipped his head, clearly uneasy. "We can escort Taron away from the farmland. The damage is done here." He paused, eyes darting from Taron to Cassandra. "But if there's more sabotage along the boundary lines, how do we prevent another outburst?"

That question hung in the smoky air. Cassandra's mind raced, the morning's events swirling. Finally, she forced a steady exhalation. "Containment," she said simply. "Keep Taron's magical usage minimal until we can check the entire network. We'll need time to break the sabotage runes safely."

Someone behind Barro muttered that time was the one luxury they didn't have, referring, no doubt, to the baron's short temper and the peasants' rising fear. Cassandra braced herself, letting the tension settle inside her. The farmland was scorched, Taron had nearly lost control again, and she was being blamed from all corners. But the sabotage was proven now, and that might be the only victory she could claim this morning.

Ulric, still standing stiffly, gestured for his men to gather. "We will ride back. Some of you remain here to oversee the scribes' work. The rest of us will escort Lord Taron back to the keep." A pointed glance at Cassandra. "You will accompany us as well, under guard."

Cassandra's throat tightened, but Taron spoke up first. "She's not a prisoner," he protested in a low, forceful tone.

Ulric regarded him coolly. "She is a suspect in a dangerous matter, Taron," he said. "And as your father, and the ruling baron, I will not tolerate unsupervised interference with the wards. You see what's at stake."

Taron's fists clenched, and Cassandra could practically feel his frustration. But she laid a hand lightly on his elbow. "Let it be," she murmured. Her voice was barely audible. "We won't solve anything by challenging him now, not with the farmland in ruins and the saboteur still free." And not with half the knights ready to pounce on any sign of disloyalty.

Reluctantly, Taron let out a ragged breath. "All right."

Taron's fists clenched so tightly that Cassandra could see the faint tremor in his forearms. But when she laid a hand lightly on his elbow, he didn't relax. Instead, he turned to her, his gaze blazing with determination. "No," he said firmly, his voice low but sharp enough to cut through the tension. "Letting it be isn't enough anymore."

Her eyes widened at the intensity in his expression, a

strength she hadn't seen so clearly before. He wasn't the man who once stood silent as his father exiled her; he was something more now—someone willing to stand and fight, not just for himself but for her as well.

Taron stepped closer, lowering his voice so only she could hear, though the weight of his words carried like thunder in her chest. "We'll convince him, Cassandra. We'll make him see your worth, even if I have to drag every knight and noble in this keep to witness what you've done. But if he won't listen..." He hesitated for only a fraction of a second, the resolve in his voice hardening. "Then we'll find another way to deal with him. I won't let him tear you down again."

Her breath caught, her hand stilling on his arm. She wasn't sure which was more startling—the fierceness in his words or the unshakable certainty in his eyes. He wasn't just angry or frustrated; he was resolute, unyielding, like a storm gathering force before it unleashed its fury.

Cassandra's voice softened, though her heart was pounding. "Taron..." she began, unsure of what to say.

He met her gaze, his own steady and unflinching. "No more waiting," he said. "No more hoping he'll come around on his own. If he refuses to see the truth, then we'll show it to everyone else. We'll expose the saboteur, rebuild the wards, prove that you belong here." His tone dipped, quieter but no less intense. "And if he still won't listen, we'll make it clear that he doesn't get to stand in our way."

For a moment, the weight of his conviction left her

speechless. She had always carried the fight for her survival on her own, her resolve steady but solitary. Now, for the first time, she saw that Taron was not only willing to fight alongside her but was ready to challenge the very foundation of his father's control if it came to that.

She nodded slowly, her fingers tightening slightly on his arm. "All right," she said softly. "But we do this carefully. We can't afford reckless moves."

A faint, grim smile touched his lips. "Carefully," he agreed. "But decisively." He glanced toward the smoldering farmland, his jaw tightening. "If my father won't protect this barony the way it should be, then I will."

Ulric seemed satisfied by that submission and turned away to address the villagers, ordering them to stay clear of the tampered posts. Taron and Cassandra retreated a few steps, while Sir Barro organized the knights. The wind gusted a swirl of ash into their faces, stinging Cassandra's eyes. Taron shielded his nose with a gloved hand and glanced around at the charred devastation.

"This is…" He swallowed, gaze haunted. "All because the wards were twisted to siphon my magic. And the people will think,"

"They'll think you lost control," Cassandra finished quietly, her own voice bleak. "And they'll blame me for not preventing it." She hesitated. "But we'll keep searching for evidence. Clearly, someone wants to incite terror. They've used your aura like a weapon." A surge of sorrow lanced through her, bridging the distance between them. She slid her gaze across his face. "I'm sorry."

"Don't," he said, despair fraying his voice. "None of this is on you."

A sharp whistle signaled that the baron's retinue was gathering to depart. The hustle of knights mounting their horses, the villagers' angry or fearful murmurs, the swirl of blackened dust, it all came together in a tableau of dread. Cassandra lifted her chin, resolving that she would not cower under suspicious glares.

Side by side, she and Taron walked to reclaim their mounts. Before she climbed astride, she paused, letting her gaze sweep the scorched farmland one last time. Even from this distance, she spotted the trailing lines of sabotage carved into the post, a dance of malicious runes that might as well have spelled her ruin. A pang of fury and heartbreak coiled in her. How easily all the trust she'd begun to build, both with Taron and the barony, was threatened by hidden saboteurs.

A knight stepped up to Cassandra's stirrup, presumably ensuring she didn't slip away. She stiffened. Taron noticed, eyes darkening. But again, she shook her head, silently pleading with him not to make a scene. The baron wanted her in chains, for all she knew. This was the lesser humiliation.

She swung up into the saddle, ignoring the cramped set of her jaw. Taron mounted alongside her; tension visible in the set of his shoulders. Behind them, Sir Barro exchanged a final word with the knights who remained to guard the farmland. Then they set off on a slow, somber ride back toward the keep.

Dust rose behind the column of horses, settling over

the scorched field like a shroud. Cassandra's stomach churned anew. She could only imagine the rumors the villagers would spread after they left: Taron nearly unleashed catastrophic magic, the wards had collapsed, farmland was destroyed under swirling arcs of power, and the witch, Cassandra, was apparently worthless at best, and traitorous at worst.

She glanced at Taron, who rode in stony silence. A hush clung to him, a reflection of his guilt and frustration. It was at that moment Cassandra realized how truly alone they might stand if the sabotage continued. Even Sir Barro, who supported them, could not quell the tide of suspicion. And Ulric had made it clear that any further destruction would be pinned on her.

Her eyes wandered to the horizon, where farmland gave way to a cluster of trees. The sabotage was more insidious than she'd imagined, striking at Taron's aura from a distance, drawing out his power while implicating them both. The baron's accusations hammered in her mind, stoking fear that maybe, even with all her skill, she couldn't protect Taron from whatever conspiracy threatened him. And if she couldn't protect him, if farmland continued to burn, how long until the baron or the people demanded an irreversible punishment?

She swallowed the lump in her throat. The weight of her old betrayal, her exile, pressed heavily on her heart, reminding her that trust was brittle. Even Taron, for all his remorse, had been powerless to save her once. She feared they might not stand a chance against sabotage now that entire fields lay in ruin.

A shifting breeze brought the smell of burnt earth again. She reached up to wipe ash from her cheek, leaving a dark smudge across the back of her hand. At her side, Taron said nothing. He occasionally glanced her way, eyes filled with an apology he had no way to articulate. Cassandra offered a faint nod, as if to say: I know. I feel it too.

They continued in tense quiet, horses trudging over the dirt road that stretched toward the keep. Sir Barro flanked them, stony-faced. Behind came half a dozen knights and a few of Ulric's courtiers, no doubt eager to swarm the baron with fresh condemnation of Cassandra's wards. At the head of the column, Ulric's posture radiated a grim certainty: He would use this fiasco to discredit Cassandra further.

She pushed away a flash of despair and forced herself to focus on what she did know. The farmland bore the same sabotage runes as inside the keep, fresh lines carved over older wards. If she and Sir Barro kept investigating, they might yet catch the culprit. But that required cooperating with a baron who loathed her. The next sabotage could happen at any moment. And Taron's aura, already raw, might not withstand many more forced meltdowns.

TWENTY-ONE

An unsteady breath quivered through her. She hadn't felt this uncertain since the day she'd first stepped back into these castle walls. Trust had begun to form between her and Taron again, but the barony's suspicion now threatened to tear that trust apart. The new wave of rumors, the farmland devastation, the baron's implied ultimatum... All were meant to undermine any faith others held in her abilities. She wondered if Taron sensed, as she did, the creeping sense that they were once more tottering on the edge of betrayal.

She recalled the trembling gratitude in Taron's eyes whenever she saved him. The night he nearly burned the orchard corridor, the moment he confessed how his father blackmailed him into silence. All those shards of closeness had begun to stitch them together. Now, with one well-placed act of sabotage, everything threatened to unravel.

Clenching the reins, Cassandra stared ahead, heart pounding. She would not be driven away this time. She would not let Taron stand alone in guilt, and she would not let the saboteur succeed. Even if the baron caged her in his keep, she would fight tooth and nail to prove her innocence. She refused to be the scapegoat as farmland burned.

Taron cast her a sidelong look, so full of questions that her breath caught. She answered him only with the faintest inclination of her head, a silent vow that she would not abandon him. Something in his eyes flickered with acknowledgment, grief, and raw determination.

They pressed onward, the keep's distant parapets coming into view against the pale sunrise. None of the knights spoke. Hoofbeats thudded in a grim drumbeat. The farmland behind them smoldered in sorrowful arcs. Cassandra's mind churned with the sabotage runes she'd seen, the baron's scathing remarks, the tight coil of Taron's magic.

By the time they reached the keep's gates, the tension had grown thick enough to taste. Within hours, the peasants would know the truth of what had transpired, or some distorted version of it: that Taron's magic once again lashed out, that Cassandra's wards came too late or not at all, that farmland was left in desolation.

As knights dismounted, Cassandra stayed astride a moment longer, trying to steady her racing thoughts. Sir Barro sent her an encouraging glance, as if to say he would keep investigating. She offered him a tight nod. She was more grateful for his loyalty than she could express, but gratitude alone wouldn't dispel her fear.

She slid down from her mare. Taron did the same,

landing lightly, though his knees bent as if drained. She reached to steady him automatically but paused when she felt eyes upon them: watchers perched on the keep's walkway, a cluster of servants peering from behind the courtyard pillars. Any sign of closeness between them might fuel more gossip.

Still, Taron didn't move away. Perhaps he was past caring how it looked. Grim-faced knights stepped forward to gather around Cassandra like a subtle guard. Her jaw tightened. It was an unsubtle reminder that she was not free to slip away. She pressed her lips together and inhaled. She felt Taron shift closer, as if stifling the impulse to speak, to protest. But he remained silent, pinned by the memory of how the baron threatened them both.

Baron Ulric strode to the front, commanding the courtyard's attention. He gave brisk instructions to a steward on assembling scribes for farmland ward analysis. Then he turned those steely eyes on Cassandra. "You, with me," he said, glancing at Taron. "And you will rest, my son. Your aura is too volatile to roam freely."

Taron clenched his jaw. "I'm not a prisoner in my own home."

"You nearly burned half the farmland. You have no idea how many fearful villagers might call for," Ulric bit off the words, emotion flickering in his face. "Just remain in the keep until that sabotage is removed. Understood?"

Taron's expression twisted, but he exhaled a shaky breath. "Fine," he said at last, voice laced with bitten-back fury. "Since you won't let me help fix this." He turned to Cassandra, eyes anguished. "Be careful."

She nodded, too weary to muster a spoken reply. Then she watched Taron stalk away across the courtyard, heading for the interior corridors, the echoes of his footsteps fading into the hush. Her heart contracted. She loathed seeing him forced into compliance like this, terrified that every meltdown would be used as proof of his danger. And she knew all too well that the baron might leverage that fear yet again.

Cassandra drew herself up, turning to meet Ulric's chilly stare. "What will you have of me, my lord?" she asked quietly. Another wave of anger and exhaustion pressed on her, yet she refused to show weakness.

"You will accompany these knights to your chamber," Ulric said, cold and brisk. "Remain there until we send for you. And do not think of vanishing into some secret corridor in the meantime. I will not tolerate any further excuse if Taron's aura flares again."

Her pulse pounded, but she dipped her head in what she hoped appeared a gesture of grudging compliance. A half-dozen knights surrounded her, ready to escort her as though she were a criminal. She noticed Sir Barro hovering uncertainly, wanting to intervene but forced to follow orders. She gave him a small nod of reassurance. They both knew the farmland sabotage had turned the situation dire, and if Cassandra tried to argue in front of everyone, it would only inflame mistrust.

She fell into step with the knights, letting them lead her toward the keep's interior. Every stride felt heavier than the last. The corridor walls rose around her like a cage, every torch sconce casting flickering shadows that reminded her of Taron's earlier meltdown. She couldn't erase the memory of his tightened jaw, his voice breaking with regret.

He faced condemnation from every angle, and she stood right beside him in the crosshairs. The sabotage, the farmland's devastation, the baron's accusations, each had driven another wedge into a fragile sense of trust. She could practically feel it fracturing beneath the weight of suspicion.

As they ascended the spiraling staircase toward her chamber, bitterness coiled. She had done everything in her power to protect Taron, but the barony's collective fear overshadowed her accomplishments. Perhaps that was the saboteur's true aim: to ensure neither Taron nor Cassandra could hold the barony's confidence. If so, it was working.

At her door, the knights paused. "I'm sorry," one muttered under his breath. He was a younger recruit, eyes flicking away with an uncomfortable flush. "Orders."

She nodded. She had no anger to spare for him. Then she slipped inside, the heavy door clanging shut behind her. The bolt slid into place. Footsteps retreated, leaving at least two knights stationed outside. Cassandra pressed her back to the closed door, exhaling shakily. Her chest felt tight as a vise.

Only a sliver of morning light peeked through her chamber's small window. Everything else was shadowy and claustrophobic. She let her gaze drift over the modest bed, the worn table, the half-burned candles, mere hours ago, she'd left them behind in a rush, not anticipating the farmland meltdown that would greet her at dawn.

She sank to the edge of the bed, an ache settling in her muscles. Anger simmered close to the surface, but so did sadness. The farmland's destruction was a blow, not just to the barony's resources but to the fragile acceptance she'd tried to cultivate. The sabotage threatened to dissolve all the progress she and Taron had made. "Fractured trust," she murmured under her breath, letting the despair weigh on her shoulders.

What would happen now? She felt Taron's anguish echo in her mind, his worried eyes, his silent apology, the memory of his raw magic lashing out. She worried he would spiral under his father's condemnation, that the entire keep would call for Cassandra's removal if one more catastrophe struck. The saboteurs wanted them to be isolated, mistrusted. And in just a few swift strokes, they'd accomplished exactly that.

She closed her eyes. Even though anger roiled like a live coal in her stomach, she refused to let hopelessness claim her. She'd survived banishment once; she would survive these accusations, too. But how many more surges could Taron withstand before he broke under the guilt? How many more fields would burn before the baron demanded her head on a pike?

Her fingers curled into the blanket, recalling how Taron's hand had briefly squeezed hers in that ashen field. That fleeting gesture of solidarity stirred something inside her, a reminder that for all the blame pinned on them, they still had each other. If they worked together to unravel the sabotage, maybe they could turn the tide. She would not let the baron's wrath silence her. She would fight. For Taron's sake, for the barony's sake, and for her own.

But the memory of the farmland's smoke-choked devastation refused to fade. She saw it every time she closed her eyes: the scorched ground, the blackened posts carved with twisted runes, the uneasy stares of knights and villagers alike. Above all, she remembered Taron's surge, the scorching arcs that cut the air and nearly burned Sir Barro. As long as the sabotage persisted, Taron remained a fuse, one spark away from disaster.

Swallowing hard, Cassandra rose from the bed, pacing the short space of her chamber. The walls felt too close, as if they were pressing inward with every breath. She clenched her hands at her sides, forcing herself to calm. Soon, she would gather what little evidence she had, coordinate with Sir Barro if he could slip her any information. She would try to figure out a new approach, some means of identifying the saboteur's next move. Because sitting idle, waiting for the baron's permission, would not save Taron from another meltdown.

Still, the question reverberated: Would the barony believe her when the next crisis came? Or would they side with the baron, seeing only a witch who failed them once more? The farmland was ravaged, the rumors on the brink of spreading like wildfire. Another deep surge of uncertainty made her heart pound. She wanted to protect these people, to protect Taron from a burden that tore him apart each day. But her power alone might not be enough to quell sabotage this cunning.

A faint shuffle arose outside her door. She stiffened, half expecting the baron to burst in with a fresh tirade. But no, the door remained locked. She pressed her forehead to the cool wooden panel, exhaling slowly.

Seconds stretched into minutes. Her thoughts roiled with doubt and fury, replaying the farmland fiasco in excruciating detail. She recalled Taron's ashen face and the pang of betrayal that tightened her own chest when the baron insinuated her wards were fueling these surges. She had never felt so trapped, caught between her determination to prove sabotage and a rising tide of blame.

And Taron... She wondered what heartbreak weighed on him as he retreated to his own rooms, likely hounded by the baron's attempts to contain him. The guilt in his eyes haunted her more than the field's blackened remains. The day had begun with frantic knocks bringing dire news. It ended, she realized with a stifling sense of finality, with her locked under suspicion, Taron's magic forcibly suppressed, and farmland in ruins.

She lowered herself into the single wooden chair by the table, feeling the day's exhaustion press down until her limbs felt heavy. She closed her eyes, letting the quiet envelop her. Outside, the keep bustled with tension, no doubt. Messengers would be racing to deliver the farmland news, scribes preparing to dismantle the sabotage runes, soldiers bracing for peasant protests. And Cassandra, the once-exiled witch, was set aside behind a locked door. Helpless, at least for now.

Her eyes opened to the flicker of morning light. She drew a shaky breath. Despite the swirling gloom, one thought anchored her: she and Taron had identified the sabotage post with fresh runes. It was something tangible, a crack in the saboteur's plan. Perhaps not enough to exonerate her in the court's eyes yet, but it was a start. She would cling to that small hope and the memory of Taron's hand gripping hers, the gratitude and heartbreak rushing between them.

Eventually, she rose to fetch a battered scrap of parchment from her bedside trunk. If she was locked here, at least she could map out the farmland wards in detail, marking where sabotage was discovered. She set a stub of charcoal to the page and began sketching rough outlines, every post, every known orchard corridor, every place Taron's aura might funnel. Her hand trembled with residual anger and heartbreak, but she pressed on, determined to glean any pattern from the saboteur's approach.

Outside, footfalls periodically disturbed the hush. Twice, she heard men exchanging hushed words. She caught only fragments, "burned fields," "witch sabotage," "Baron Ulric says...", and each snippet sent a pang through her chest. Anger warred with a bone-deep exhaustion, but she forced herself to focus on the lines of her sketches.

Yes, trust lay fractured, but she wasn't powerless. For Taron and for herself, she would unravel the truth, no matter how the baron snarled. She only hoped Taron could hold out a little longer without succumbing to another surge, one that might fling him beyond Cassandra's reach.

She closed her eyes, drawing in a slow breath. The farmland fiasco had struck like a hammer blow; she could almost taste the soot on her tongue. But the saboteur had made a mistake in leaving obvious tampered runes behind. She and Sir Barro, and maybe Taron, if he could steal a moment away from his father's watch, would press forward. And if the entire barony turned on Cassandra, she would stand her ground regardless.

In the stillness of the chamber, she listened to her own heartbeat, each throb echoing the vow she quietly repeated: I won't let them tear us apart again. I won't be exiled by their fear.

Though her mind reeled with unanswered questions, her determination blazed. Outside, the day rose over blackened fields, rumors swirling on the wind. And behind that locked door, Cassandra braced herself for the storms yet to come, fiercely gripping the fragile threads of trust with Taron that, if they could endure, might save them both.

TWENTY-TWO

Cassandra had just finished marking a warding circle in a dim corridor when footsteps approached, quiet, but firm enough on the stone floor to signify a knight's measured pace. Sir Barro. She straightened, heart beating faster than she cared to admit, and stared down the hall's length. In the faint glow of mounted torches, she spotted his familiar solid frame, broad shoulders filling the corridor.

She swept a stray lock of hair from her face and tried to seem unruffled. It was late, nearly midnight by her estimation, yet the castle's corridors showed no sign of rest. Even in the hush of these shadowed halls, suspicion smoldered like banked coals. Whispers trailed her footsteps at all hours. Guards and servants alike fixed her with wary stares, as if any moment she might ignite the keep in an arc of witch-fire. A few days ago, she might have openly scowled at them. Now, she understood her energy was better spent on the real threat: the saboteurs orchestrating mayhem from the shadows, all too eager to let her take the blame.

At the distant corner, Sir Barro inclined his head in greeting. His stern face carried new lines of tension, and she wondered what fresh tidings had come to weigh on him.

"Milady," he said quietly once close enough. "I trust your last ward inspection is complete?"

"It is," she answered. "Though I suspect it won't matter if we can't root out the saboteur." She let her voice drop to a whisper. "Did anything else come to light? Another forged ledger? A runic message?"

He nodded curtly and gestured for her to follow. Without exchanging further words in the open corridor, the two of them turned down a lesser-used passage. The walls rose overhead in cramped angles, the air stale with disuse, and every step they took kicked up faint echoes. This had become their new habit: drifting through the keep's older corridors when they needed privacy, away from patrolling knights and eavesdropping staff.

When Barro found a small wooden door beneath a sconce that sputtered with half-dead flame, he tugged it open. The room beyond was more of a storage niche than a room, cobwebbed shelves and crates pressed against stone walls. He held the door for her to enter, then stepped inside and quietly shut it, leaving them with the flickering torchlight from outside as their only illumination.

"I intercepted a messenger earlier," he murmured. "Not personally, mind you. A friend among the knights flagged a letter. Its contents are...unusual."

Cassandra's throat tightened. "A letter? From whom, and to whom was it intended?"

He exhaled slowly. "We're not certain. The messenger was hired by a 'private benefactor.' Not the baron, at least not openly. But the letter bears some phrase that might interest you."

She felt a prickle of tension along her arms. "Show me."

He fished in a leather pouch at his belt and withdrew a folded scrap of parchment. Rather than offer it to her immediately, he paused, steadying his voice. "You should know that the keep is on edge about your rummaging in old records. Some of the men are convinced you plan to manipulate Taron's wards further. I do what I can to quiet them, but rumors spread faster than we can contain."

Cassandra's chest knotted with anger. "And if we do nothing, the saboteur prevails. Let them whisper."

"Agreed." Stoically, Barro handed her the parchment. "I've risked bringing this to you because it might be genuine proof. But be cautious, if you're caught with it, they'll accuse you of forging it yourself."

She accepted the parchment gently. "Understood."

Unfolding the letter, she had to squint in the dim light. Sir Barro struck a small flint off the stone, lighting a stub of candle that he produced from a saddlebag. The cramped space became marginally brighter.

Her eyes scanned the words. At first, the letter seemed an ordinary business note:

Payment for special deliveries needed. Ensure readiness by next feast-day. Our consultant demands precision with the wards; inefficiencies will not be tolerated.

But the final lines caught her attention:

Black Sigils are prepared for the final strike. Must align with the next meltdown, or sabotage is wasted. Confirm infiltration success. Burn this missive.

Cassandra's heart lurched at the phrase Black Sigils. That alone battered her composure. She'd heard rumors of them in old texts: runic devices capable of undermining magical wards from within, unleashing raw magic in uncontrollable bursts. If anyone had found a way to replicate them, Taron's surges would be tenfold more lethal.

She dragged her gaze lower. The more she read, the more her pulse hammered. "This is as bad as I feared," she whispered, voice rasping. "It means the saboteur, and possibly more than one, has a direct plan to trigger Taron's next meltdown. And they intend to time it with these… horrid things."

Barro nodded grimly. "We have to assume the saboteur is close. They must be feeding every detail about Taron's wards, or how else could they plan that precisely?"

Cassandra inhaled. "Who else knows about this letter?"

"Only me, and now you." He took a guarded step back, nerves etched on his brow. "My friend turned it over without reading it. I swore I'd keep his name quiet to avoid repercussions."

She folded the letter carefully, her mind churning. "We can't let them bury this. But presenting it to the baron? He might dismiss it outright, or worse, accuse me of inventing it."

Barro's lips pressed to a thin line. "Or the baron might pretend ignorance while concealing his own knowledge."

Cassandra didn't need reminding that Baron Ulric had repeatedly refused to believe sabotage was real, unless it served him to do so. And Taron's father had grown colder since so much farmland had been scorched. Would he be so ruthless as to conspire with outsiders? She shook that suspicion aside for now, focusing on the immediate threat. "I need to cross-check references to these Black Sigils," she said, voice hushed. "If there's a reference in the old archives about how they target wards, I might find a clue to counter them."

Barro studied her. "I can distract the guards near the library's main hall. But you'll have to move quietly. Word is the steward himself has begun keeping watch on the archives at the baron's command, to catch you if you so much as open a ledger."

The thought of being cornered by suspicious stewards or knights chilled her. Every corridor in the keep seemed to have eyes now. Even so, she had no choice. "Tell me when," she said.

"In one hour. That should allow me time to redirect tomorrow's guard shift rosters. With luck, you'll slip in unnoticed for at least a short while."

She nodded. Before slipping the parchment into her belt pouch, she pressed it to her chest, eyes roving the cramped storage niche, as though half expecting a spy to jump out from behind the crates. "Thank you," she said, quiet but sincere. "You're risking yourself for this."

Barro's stern expression softened a fraction. "I do it because Taron trusts you. And...because I've seen enough to know you're not behind these attacks. I'd be a fool to let the real traitor roam free."

That simple statement of faith sent a hush of relief through her. She extended her hand, letting it brush his gauntleted forearm in a rare gesture of gratitude. He inclined his head in response. Then he turned away, leaving behind the small candle for her.

The moment he opened the door, the dim torchlight spilled across them again. "I'll meet you in the corridor by the tapestry of the green stag," he said quietly. "In an hour."

Her heart twisted. "I'll be there."

He slipped out, footsteps receding quickly. Cassandra stood alone; the hush thick around her. She glanced at the flickering candle again, pressed a palm briefly to her belt pouch, feeling that damning letter, and exhaled. A final strike. They were planning to unleash Taron's magic in some catastrophic event far worse than farmland devastation. And if the saboteur timed it precisely, they might destroy half the keep. Or else provoke Taron into harming so many that exiling him or executing him became unstoppable.

She must act fast.

TWENTY-THREE

An hour later, her heart pounded as she wove through the keep's darkened corridors, each footstep measured to avoid echoing. Tory sconces had been turned low for the night, casting restless shadows at every corner. As she slipped past a yawning guard stationed at a side entrance, she silently praised whatever distraction Sir Barro had orchestrated to keep him from paying close attention.

She found him in the corridor near the tapestry of the green stag, as promised. He nodded but said nothing, instead jerking his chin in the direction of the old library wing. She nodded back, letting him lead.

They passed no one else in the hall; presumably, Barro had contrived some emergency farther upstairs. She could almost sense the tension in his body as he guided her, sword clutched in one hand, posture rigid.

Soon they reached the library's antechamber. A deserted reading desk stood near the entry, its stack of loose quills and inkwells suggesting a clerk typically monitored who entered. Tonight, no clerk or steward. Perfect.

Barro paused, glancing behind them once more. Satisfied by the silence, he motioned for Cassandra to proceed. "I'll stand guard here, keep an ear out."

She squeezed his wrist gently. "Thank you." Then she ducked inside, taking care not to let the heavy door creak too loudly.

The library was dark, save for a single candelabra perched at the far end near a row of shelves. The hush was absolute, broken only by the faint rasp of her own breath. She moved deeper, eyes adjusting to faint lamplight that reached from the antechamber. Endless rows of leather-bound tomes and scrolls presented themselves, the faint smell of parchment and dust swirling in the still air.

She had studied the library's layout before, mentally mapping the location of different sections: general history in the center shelves, ledgers and accounts toward the left alcove, arcane references shelved along the library's back wall. That was her real target: the old wards and runic texts.

As she navigated the labyrinth of shelves, her mind roiled with the phrase Black Sigils. She recalled fragments from her training with Miriana: references to an ancient device that could unravel wards from within, effectively turning protective magic into a destructive force. If the saboteur had indeed found or replicated such runes, Taron's wards, even with her help, could be forcibly corrupted.

Silently, she slid out a thick tome from a shelf labeled "Runic Anomalies, Extinct or Forbidden." The leather binding squeaked in protest, dust drifting off in a swirl. Wincing at the small sound, she ducked into an alcove behind the shelves. The alcove was cramped but offered partial cover. She balanced the book on her knees, using the candle stub from earlier.

Page after page, she scanned references to malignant wards, cursed sigils. None quite matched what she needed. On the next page, though, her breath caught:

...Black Sigils, rumored to manipulate deep ley energy, forcibly amplifying a caster's surges. Historically invoked in times of war to turn an enemy mage's power against them. Surviving records are scant, as most references were destroyed by decree of the Crown centuries ago...

Her heart thumped. So, it was real. She read on:

These sigils, once activated, latch onto existing wards. Their effect is subtle until the final moment of synergy when the mage's aura is forcibly unbalanced. Historians speculate that only those with inside knowledge of the mage's ward structure can place the sigils effectively...

Inside knowledge. A chill skittered down her spine. Taron's wards, both personal and keep-based, were no trivial matter. She had re-etched them herself. The saboteur would need details from someone intimately aware of those wards. Or from someone who'd learned such details over time. Cassandra's hands trembled around the page. Could it be that the sabotage was not the work of a random rogue agent, but rather someone in the baron's upper circle?

She pushed on, trying to glean how to counter them:

...Little recorded on how to neutralize the Sigils once anchored. A conjurer's best hope is to sever the Sigils from the ward matrix before the meltdown can spark. Failing that, the meltdown often proves fatal to the mage or those caught in the radius.

Her stomach twisted painfully. Not only was time of the essence, but there might be no easy fix if the saboteur had already placed even one such Sigil. For a moment, her eyes burned with worry. She thought of Taron, his haunted expression, the way his power flared unpredictably under stress, how close he'd come to losing control in the farmland fiasco.

She slid the tome back. Although she yearned to keep reading, she couldn't remain there forever. She needed to see if any other volumes or archived documents referenced the sabotage's method. Carefully, she slipped through the rows of shelves, scanning more titles. Each second she lingered invited discovery, but she couldn't leave yet. They needed every detail if they were to survive this conspiracy.

A faint scrape sounded behind her, wood against stone. Cassandra froze, heart pounding. The library door? Fear spiked, but she forced herself into action, ducking between shelves stacked high with musty tomes. She extinguished her candle stub with a quick pinch of her fingers, willing herself not to yelp at the tiny burn. Darkness enfolded her.

Footsteps, light but deliberate, crossed the library threshold. Someone had entered. She pressed herself flush to the shelf, breath caught in her lungs. Through the gloom, she glimpsed a silhouette: tall, hooded, moving with uncanny quiet. For an agonizing moment, she feared it might be one of the saboteurs. But then she caught a faint glimmer of runic metal at the person's wrist, some kind of cuff?

Her mind conjured a hundred possibilities. She stifled the impulse to run. The figure advanced deeper, scanning the shelves with slow, measured intent. Cassandra bit her lip. She looked around for an escape route. The only other exit from the library's far side was boarded up from disuse, and she had no illusions about prying it open quietly. No, she'd have to stay hidden or slip behind the intruder, if the chance arose.

But the figure headed for the back corner, toward the same arcane references she'd just abandoned. Cassandra felt her heart lurch. If they saw the tome out of place, or discovered her presence... She clenched her fists, forcing herself not to panic. She had no weapon beyond a small piece of ward chalk in her belt pouch. And that letter, the one referencing Black Sigils, sat precariously on her person. If this intruder discovered it...

More footsteps. Then a faint rustle, a drawer opening, or a hidden compartment? Cassandra couldn't see from her angle. Her lungs burned with the need to breathe more deeply, but she held back. She heard soft rummaging, the crinkle of parchment. Was this person stashing documents in the library? Or searching for them?

Finally, after what felt like an eternity, the figure stood abruptly. Cassandra risked a tiny shift to see them turning away, a folded parchment now in their gloved hand, faint candlelight glinting off the edge. They pivoted, heading for the door again. She braced for any sign that they sensed her presence. One misstep, and she might be forced into a confrontation.

But the intruder neither paused nor surveyed the shelves more thoroughly. With the same eerie silence, they recrossed the library, exiting into the corridor. The door clicked shut behind them.

Cassandra exhaled shakily, tension flooding her limbs. She waited a few moments longer, straining her ears for any shuffle of steps or voices outside. Nothing. She stepped from behind the shelf, eyes darting toward that back corner. Should she investigate? It was reckless, yet the intruder's presence here couldn't be chance.

She glided across the library, scanning the shelves. One drawer near the floor was slightly ajar, which she didn't recall leaving that way. She crouched, carefully sliding it fully open. Inside lay a scattering of scrolls. She lifted one, but it seemed only a battered treatise on farmland wards. Beneath it, a few blank parchments. Nothing obviously incriminating. Perhaps the intruder had removed something rather than depositing it.

Her breath came in jagged gulps. She considered rummaging more thoroughly but realized time was slipping away. Sir Barro might be in danger if the intruder passed him in the corridor. Worse, if a watchful guard returned, they might find her crouched here, letter in hand. She shut the drawer, resolving to share this with Taron once she was safe outside of the library. Maybe he'd recognize the significance of the drawer's contents or recall which references were missing.

With that plan fraying her nerves, she hurried toward the exit. The corridor outside was silent, except for Sir Barro standing tensely near the reading desk, sword half-drawn.

"All well?" he asked under his breath when she emerged.

"Someone came in," she whispered, consciousness prickling with worry. "Tall, hooded. They found a hidden drawer. Took something."

Barro's eyes flashed. "They left here not a minute ago. I heard footsteps but couldn't see who it was, someone must have used the side passage to slip in and away."

Her mind churned. She had to warn Taron at once, show him the new letter. Everything pointed to a deeper infiltration than they'd suspected. "Let's get out of here," she murmured.

CHAPTER

TWENTY-FOUR

They parted ways in a discreet corridor. Barro claimed he'd handle any follow-up interrogation if a steward demanded to know why the library's antechamber was empty. Cassandra thanked him again, then hurried down a winding flight of stone steps leading to the keep's lower level. She'd hide the letter somewhere safe or at least keep it until she could speak directly with Taron.

But as she descended, a swirl of memories crowded her thoughts: farmland scorched, sabotage runes discovered, Taron's meltdown that nearly cost them all. The keep simmered with tension. She couldn't help replaying the intruder's silhouette in her mind. Why retrieve a parchment from the library at this hour, unless it carried crucial secrets about wards? The sabotage seemed orchestrated from inside these walls, yet by whom?

By the time she reached her chamber corridor, she realized she couldn't simply lock herself away for the night. She needed Taron's counsel, and more than that, she wanted his presence, the sense that they fought side by side, not torn by suspicion. Her cheeks warmed at the memory of the last time they'd made love. The rumors might brand them both reckless, but she didn't care. If anything, each passing crisis only underscored how deeply their fates were entwined.

She could still feel the heat of his breath on her skin, the way his lips had claimed hers with a hunger that stole her breath. Every kiss had been an unspoken apology, a promise, and a plea. She remembered the way his hands had trembled when they first slid over her shoulders, as though he feared she might pull away. But she hadn't. She'd let him undress her, each layer stripped away with a reverence that made her heart ache.

That night, they had moved with quiet urgency, as if the world outside his chamber didn't exist. She remembered the way he whispered her name like it was sacred, the way his touch explored her as though memorizing every detail. His magic had flared faintly as they came together, not in chaos but in harmony, a warm hum that thrummed in the air between them. And in the aftermath, as they lay tangled together, his arms around her, she had felt for the first time that his walls had truly fallen, leaving nothing but vulnerability and trust between them.

The rumors might brand them both reckless, but she didn't care. Let the whispers swirl through the halls; let the nobles spin their stories. If anything, each passing crisis only underscored how deeply their fates were entwined.

Gathering her courage, she pivoted, heading instead toward the library's upper floors. Taron sometimes spent his late evenings in the smaller library alcove closer to his personal study, cross-referencing old warding texts with the bits of sabotage evidence they'd already gathered. Half the time, he was beset by guards or his father's demands, but tonight, Cassandra suspected he'd steal a vigil in some quiet corner.

She navigated the labyrinth of hallways, careful to avoid the main passages, where patrolling knights might question her. Tapestries with baronial crests fluttered overhead in the occasional draft. At last, she reached a narrower gallery lined with dusty portraits. The final door on the left led to a seldom-used reading alcove Taron favored.

Sure enough, a faint glow pooled beneath that door. Cassandra pressed her ear to the wood. Silence. She pushed it open with cautious quiet.

Inside, Taron was seated at a small table, quill in hand, a large tome spread before him. A single hooded lantern flickered near his elbow, casting his features into shifting light and shadow. He looked up at once, tension etched on the set of his jaw. But the moment he recognized her, relief flickered in his hazel eyes.

"Cassandra," he breathed, standing quickly. "I, I was hoping you'd come."

She shut the door behind her, pressing her spine to the wood. For a moment, she just observed him: the lines of fatigue marking his handsome face, the faint scorch mark near his left wrist where a meltdown had singed him days ago. His shock of dark hair fell across his forehead, reminding her of how close they'd been the last time she siphoned off his power.

"You're up late," she murmured, stepping forward. "Cross-referencing something?"

He nodded and gestured to the spread of papers on the table, frustration tightening his features. "I found an old mention of sabotage wards used in a past barony conflict. I'm trying to see if they align with the runes we discovered near my corridor. It's... not going well." He exhaled, then looked her over carefully. "What of you? Were you with Barro again?"

She set her belt pouch on the table. "Yes, and we found something. A letter referencing...Black Sigils." Her voice trembled slightly at the word. She met his gaze, aware of how the mention might startle him.

Indeed, Taron's hand tightened around the edge of the table, color draining from his cheeks. "Black Sigils? I've read only rumors. They're, dangerous beyond measure."

"Sir Barro intercepted a letter that said the Sigils are ready for a 'final strike.' They want to trigger it during your next big surge." She forced her voice not to quake, though dread coiled inside her. "We suspect someone here is funneling them knowledge of your wards."

His eyes narrowed. "Then, someone must have access to extremely private details. Details only the baron or his closest council might know."

A dull ache spread in her chest at the mention of the baron. She'd long suspected he was involved with some underhanded dealings. But this?

Reaching into the pouch, she withdrew the folded missive. Carefully, she held it out. Taron studied it under the lantern's glow, eyes sweeping over the lines. With each phrase, his jaw clenched tighter.

"Burn this missive," he read softly, the final instruction. Then he lifted his gaze to hers. "So, Barro's friend prevented that from happening?"

"Yes." Cassandra sat beside him, shoulders brushing in the cramped space. "And that's not all. I saw an intruder in the main library tonight, rummaging in a hidden drawer. I couldn't see who it was, it was too dark. But they left with some parchment. Could be instructions, or more details on your wards, or... I don't know." She shivered. "Whoever it was moved with purpose, Taron. They weren't just snooping."

He set the letter down, one hand fisting so tight his knuckles whitened. "And these lines about infiltration... someone's obviously making me appear out of control, fueling the rumor that you're the saboteur." His voice cracked with anger. "If we don't trace this network soon, the next meltdown might be unstoppable."

They fell silent. Cassandra reached for the crumpled scroll he'd been perusing before her arrival. She saw runic sketches, scrawling notes in Taron's surprisingly neat handwriting. Her gaze lifted to his taut profile. "I looked up references to the Black Sigils in a different volume. They latch onto a target's wards from inside. If we can't isolate where they're placed, the meltdown will be near impossible to prevent."

Taron's frustration crackled through the air. "So, we

need to know each ward's status intimately, and root out any hidden runes. That's a lot of ground to cover in the keep alone, not to mention farmland and other outbuildings."

"Yes. And we must do it discreetly, or the saboteur will accelerate their plan."

He sank wearily onto the table's edge, half-sitting, half-standing. "This conspiracy...my father's refusal to see reason...Cassandra, it's all building toward something catastrophic. I can sense it. I just," His breathing hitched. "I can't lose control again, not if it kills half the keep."

Without thinking, she placed her hand on his forearm, feeling the warmth of his body through the fabric. "We'll stop it," she said softly. "I won't let them twist your magic like that."

He turned his hand over, letting their palms meet in a gentle clasp. A swirl of emotion churned in his eyes, fear, guilt, and something else that brushed the edges of longing. Cassandra's pulse fluttered. In that tenuous moment, it no longer mattered that they were tethered by old betrayals and fresh dangers. They were two souls bracing against a storm, each the other's only lifeline.

She withdrew slightly, remembering the letter. "We should see if there's any clue in these phrases. You mentioned infiltration...did anything about the wording strike you as familiar?"

Taron shuffled the parchment once more, then froze, his gaze snagging on a specific turn of phrase near the top. He tapped it. "Here, it speaks of needing 'precision with the wards...no margin for trifling theatrics...' Something like that. That's almost exactly how my father once worded his demands in a private letter to me, back before you returned."

Her throat felt suddenly tight. "You think he...?"

Taron's voice came out a bare murmur, as though the admission pained him. "My father wrote me often about controlling my magic. If I read that letter side by side with some of his old demands, I'd bet the phrasing is identical. He's always used that exact phrase, 'no margin for trifling theatrics', when scolding me about wards."

The air between them tensed. A swirl of anger flared in Taron's eyes, and for a heartbeat, Cassandra thought of how fiercely he fought to earn that man's approval, only to find possible betrayal behind it. Baron Ulric had always seemed single-minded in forcing Taron's aura under control. Was it unthinkable that he might be feeding information to a Baron Felstain, or at least to conspirators, hoping to orchestrate a meltdown that pinned blame squarely on Cassandra?

Taron set the letter down. He slammed his fist against the edge of the table, the wood groaning under the force. "This is outrageous," he snarled, his voice cutting through the tense air. His other hand fisted tightly around the letter, his knuckles white, the parchment crumpling under his grip. The flicker of magic that radiated from him was barely restrained, sending faint tremors through the lanterns. "If my father has a hand in this—if he's the one feeding them information about my wards—it's not just betrayal. It's treason against his own blood, against the barony."

He rose to his feet abruptly, the movement sharp, almost violent, as though sitting still might suffocate him. His chest heaved with fury, and his jaw was set so tightly that Cassandra could see the strain in the muscles of his neck. "For years, I've fought to control this magic, to keep it from consuming me, and all the while, *he* might have been sabotaging my every effort. Using me. Manipulating you. And for what? To tighten his grip on the barony? To cast you out again? To punish us both for something we never did?"

"Taron," Cassandra began, her voice quiet but steady, "we don't know for certain. We—"

"We know enough," he snapped, turning toward her. But his anger wasn't directed at her—it burned for the man who had dominated their lives for so long. His eyes met hers, and she saw the depth of his anguish, the fire of his determination. "The wording in that letter isn't a coincidence, Cassandra. It's him. It has to be. Who else would have this level of access, this much control? And if he thinks I'm just going to stand by while he plays games with our lives, he's sorely mistaken."

Cassandra felt her breath catch at the raw intensity in his voice. She had seen him angry before, even furious, but never like this, with this much unbridled strength and resolve. It was as though all the years of guilt, fear, and hesitation had been burned away, leaving behind someone unyielding and fiercely protective.

Taron began pacing, his magic crackling faintly in the air. "We'll confront him," he said, his voice gaining strength with every word. "If he's behind this, he doesn't get to hide in the shadows. He doesn't get to smear your name, orchestrate sabotage, and then sit back while we take the fall. If he's working with these people, we'll expose him. To the council, to the knights, to the entire barony if we have to."

His pacing halted, and he turned to face her fully. The intensity in his gaze pinned her in place. "But if he's too entrenched—if his power in the court is too strong—we'll find another way to stop him. Together." His voice dropped, softer but no less resolute. "I'm not letting him destroy us again. Not you. Not me. Not this barony."

Cassandra swallowed hard, the weight of his words settling over her. She had spent years fighting her battles alone, but now, she had someone willing to take on the storm with her, someone who wouldn't hesitate to stand against his own blood for the truth. Her chest tightened with something she couldn't quite name—gratitude, admiration, and something deeper, something she wasn't ready to voice.

She reached out, her fingers brushing against his. "If we're going to do this," she said quietly, "we have to be smart about it. Your father is dangerous, Taron. You've seen what he's capable of. We can't let him corner us."

Taron's hand closed over hers, his grip strong and steady. "We won't," he promised. His voice was softer now, but no less fierce. "I've spent my whole life letting him control me, making me doubt myself. But not anymore. If he's behind this, if he's betrayed us, he'll face the consequences. And this time, Cassandra, I'll make sure he never touches you—or me—again.

TWENTY-FIVE

Cassandra's heart gave a painful squeeze at the raw betrayal in his voice. She squeezed his arm gently. "We don't know everything yet," she tried to soothe him. "It might be that he used the same turn of phrase, and the writer borrowed it. But the coincidence is terrifying. Where else would they glean inside knowledge about your wards?"

His breathing quickened with an undercurrent of fury. "He's the one who insisted you be the scapegoat from the beginning. He refused to see sabotage even when we brought him evidence. Now this letter hints at infiltration from the baron's highest vantage." He shoved a hand through his hair, making it stand at odd angles. "Damn him, Cassandra. If he truly helped them gather details..."

She placed a bracing hand on his shoulder, feeling the tension in his muscles. "We'll find out. More importantly, we'll put a stop to it. We have to. If the saboteur times these Sigils with your meltdown, the entire keep, everyone in it, will be in unimaginable danger."

His gaze flickered to her; expression etched with conflict. "Why do you keep risking yourself for this? For me?"

The question sent a wave of emotion through her chest. Memories fluttered behind her eyes: the lonely forest nights, her bitterness over his past silence, the unstoppable warmth she still felt whenever he looked at her. She fought a tremor in her voice. "Because your magic doesn't define you," she said simply. "Because I see the man who tries so hard not to harm a single person, even at the cost of yourself. And because, despite what they all whisper, I know you'd never let me stand alone in danger."

He swallowed, blinking heavily, as though her words hit him deeper than he expected. After a beat, he reached for the quill again, but only to set it aside. His free hand found hers once more on the table's surface. The hush around them seemed to intensify.

"We're in this together," he said, almost a whisper. "And if my father truly betrays us...I won't let him succeed. I won't let him destroy you."

A quiver rose in her throat. She parted her lips to respond, but no words formed. The swirl of candlelight caught the angle of his jaw. She realized how close they were in the cramped alcove, the table's corner pressing into her hip, Taron's breath warming the air between them.

Taron's hand came up, brushing against her cheek with a touch so gentle it made her chest ache. His fingers lingered, tracing the line of her jaw as though he needed to memorize her face. His voice, when he spoke, was stronger now, steady and filled with a conviction that sent a shiver down her spine. "I mean it, Cassandra. I don't care what it costs me. I won't let him take you from me again. Not your name, not your place here, and not... us."

Her breath caught, her heart thundering at the weight of his words. The intensity in his gaze pinned her in place, his eyes searching hers as if daring her to challenge his promise. But she didn't—she couldn't. All she could see was the depth of his determination, the quiet, fierce love that he no longer seemed willing to hide.

"We'll fight him together," he continued, his voice firm now, as though the words themselves were armor. "And if we can't change his mind, then we'll find another way. I'll face whatever I have to, Cassandra, but I won't lose you again."

Her lips trembled, and the quiver in her throat rose higher, threatening to spill over. "Taron..." she whispered, her voice barely audible, laden with emotion. She wasn't sure what she was about to say—gratitude, caution, a desperate plea for him to be careful—but before she could find the words, he leaned in.

The distance between them disappeared in an instant, and his lips found hers with a slow, deliberate tenderness that stole her breath. The table's edge pressed into her hip, but she barely noticed, her senses consumed by him—the warmth of his mouth, the way his hand slid into her hair, anchoring her to him as though she were the only solid thing in his world. The kiss deepened, his other hand curving around her waist, pulling her closer until the space between them was nothing but a memory.

Cassandra's hands rose of their own accord, her fingers tangling in the fabric of his tunic as though afraid he might slip away. But Taron wasn't going anywhere. Every touch, every press of his lips, every shift of his body against hers spoke of unwavering resolve, of promises unspoken yet unmistakable. The frustration and fear from moments before melted away, replaced by a certainty that settled deep in her chest.

When they finally broke apart, their foreheads rested together, their breaths mingling in the warm, candlelit air. Taron's hands stayed on her, one cradling the back of her neck, the other still at her waist, as if letting her go would break him.

"You mean everything to me," he murmured, his voice raw and honest. "Whatever comes, whatever we have to face, I'll fight for you, Cassandra. For us."

Her throat tightened, and she swallowed hard, her fingers still clutching his tunic. "You don't have to fight alone," she whispered. "I'm here, Taron. I've always been here."

His lips curved into a faint smile, one that softened the intensity in his expression but didn't diminish the strength behind it. "I know," he said. "And I won't take that for granted. Not ever again."

As much as Cassandra wanted to stay in Taron's arms, to let the warmth of his embrace and the strength in his promises shield her from the storm raging around them, she knew they couldn't linger here. The saboteur was still out there, the Black Sigils poised for their next strike, and every moment they spent wrapped in each other risked giving their enemies more ground. Reluctantly, she drew back, her hands slipping from his chest though her fingers ached to stay.

"We need to focus," she said softly, her voice steady despite the tightness in her throat. "There's too much at stake to lose sight of what we're fighting for." She held his gaze for a moment longer, letting the conviction in his eyes steady her resolve, then turned back toward the table, ready to dive into the grim work ahead. "We should check every single corridor ward, every farmland post, and do it quietly. Sir Barro will help. We can't rely on official channels."

He dipped his head in agreement. "And we'll monitor my father's messages. If he's passing more information, something might slip."

A flicker of hope stirred in her chest amid the tension. They had a plan, albeit a precarious one. She could almost forget the haunted look Taron wore whenever another meltdown threatened to devour him. Yet the fresh mention of these Sigils worsened the stakes. Time was short, and the final strike could be mere days or hours away.

She slid closer, turning so that their shoulders brushed, scanning the letter once more. "We can start tomorrow night," she said, forcing her voice to steadiness. "I'll say I'm reapplying wards. No one questions me doing that, though they assume I might sabotage them. Barro can run interference to keep the suspicious knights away."

He nodded. "And I'll talk to a few guards loyal to me, they might pass word if the baron tries to schedule any unusual deliveries or hold private summits with unknown visitors."

Warm air fanned across Cassandra's cheek as Taron leaned in to point out a portion of the letter. She caught the faint scent of soap and the tang of leather from his coat. Even in the midst of danger, that closeness sent her heart racing. The hush became almost reverent as they studied each scrap of coded words, each possibility to block the saboteur's next move. It felt like hours, though only minutes passed, their whispered conversation building a fragile framework of how they might save the barony from a cunning infiltration.

At one point, Taron rubbed a hand over his face, weariness etched in every line of his posture. "I'm sorry," he murmured, voice thick with guilt. "All you've endured, and still...this is all so heavy."

She set the letter aside, turning more fully to face him. "I chose to come back rather than letting your father's threats harm my fellow witches. And now, seeing the sabotage, I can't walk away." Her throat bobbed. "Don't apologize for a battle we must fight together."

He met her gaze, his eyes reflecting the lantern's glow. Silver flecks shimmered in the hazel depths. Heat flared in Cassandra's cheeks. She remembered every harrowing surge she'd stabilized, every time he'd nearly collapsed in her arms. The tension in the air was suddenly charged with more than their conspiratorial urgency.

He drew a careful breath. "Whatever happens, Cassandra, I'm grateful you're still here." The words trembled with sincerity. "I won't let them destroy you, or us."

That single syllable, us, slipped past his lips with surprising boldness. Her heart stuttered. Then Taron lifted the corner of the parchment again, as if needing a distraction. She laid her hand atop it, stopping him gently.

"There'll be time to read it again," she said, voice hushed. "For now, we both need rest. We can't face tomorrow exhausted out of our wits. The saboteur will be at full strength, and we can't afford a mistake."

He nodded, though reluctance flickered in his gaze. "You're right."

They shared a glance that seemed to speak volumes. Slowly, Taron placed the letter aside, out of immediate view. And then, in a small breath of quiet, he took Cassandra's other hand, both of hers now cradled in his own. Heat pulsed through that touch, a low hum of connection that neither entirely masked nor spoke aloud.

The lantern's flame danced across the stony walls. She felt a tremor work its way through her chest, the night's revelations pounding in her veins. So many dangers threatened to tear them apart, but in this dim alcove, in the perfect hush of these moments, it felt as though they had forged a fragile stronghold all their own. The final strike approached, sabotage closed in, and her name hung poised at the tip of every suspicious tongue in the keep. And still, Taron was here, pressing warmth into her hands.

His gaze held a question she couldn't quite decipher, but she suspected it hovered on the boundary between fear and longing. Then, carefully, so carefully, he let one hand drift across the table's surface until it found hers again, their fingers tangling in silent promise. The hush around them swelled, charged with everything that remained unspoken.

She drew in a breath that quivered. And in that poised silence, his hand slid fully around her own, as if to keep her anchored to him, wordlessly reminding her that some bonds, even amid all this cunning manipulation, could endure.

TWENTY-SIX

Cassandra stepped out into the moonlit courtyard, her pulse thudding in her ears despite the hush of the late hour. Gravel crunched beneath her boots, and above, the sky unfurled in a tapestry of stars. Yet no glow of starlight could veil the foreboding that curled through her chest. She sensed Taron's presence behind her, a guarded warmth at her back. Together, they navigated the courtyard's uneven stones, guided by rumors that might finally unmask the turncoat knight rumored to be near the old watchtower.

Only a sparse handful of torches still burned this deep into the night, flickering against the fortress wall. Their shadows stretched across the ground, merging every so often in a dance of uncertain shapes. Cassandra found herself glancing warily at the corners of the yard, half-expecting a cloaked figure to dart from behind the wooden cart or the large water trough near the stable yard gates.

She caught Taron's reflection in a shallow puddle, the

ripple of water distorting his somber expression. His hand twitched at his side, and she knew the tension in him was building, anxiety that if he lost control of his power, the entire keep could be swallowed in chaos. He was a living conduit of arcane force, one that conspirators sought to weaponize. The farmland sabotage had proven how far the saboteurs would go. A ragged knot of anger and protectiveness seized Cassandra's throat. She would not let them win.

"Do you sense anything?" Taron asked softly, sidling closer. His dark hair brushed the collar of his coat, and moonlight slid across the faint lines of worry on his face.

Cassandra shook her head, scanning the yard. "Not yet," she murmured. "Sir Barro said he'd intercept any watchers posted near the tower. We should meet him at the rampart staircase."

Taron exhaled, nodding. The tension of the past days, clashes with the baron, the farmland fiasco, and the near-constant accusations against Cassandra, had weighed on him like a millstone. Usually, he tried not to reveal how deeply it wore him down, but tonight his brow remained creased with both worry and the flicker of raw magic. She could almost see the sparks itching to break free beneath the gloves he wore.

They advanced toward the tower's silhouette looming at the outer edge of the keep. It rose against the night sky, half in ruin, used so rarely that many claimed it was haunted. More likely, Cassandra thought it was simply neglected, a perfect place for clandestine meetings.

A faint scuff on the stones made her whirl. Her hand

shot to the belt pouch containing her warding chalk: a reflex sharpened by countless nights of sabotage hunts. But a familiar figure stepped from the gloom: Sir Barro. His helmet was tucked under one arm, and the faint torchlight revealed the set of his hard jaw.

"You're on time," he greeted them quietly. "No sign of the knight yet, but my men are stationed beyond the eastern arch. If he's coming with reinforcements, we'll know."

Cassandra nodded. "Thanks for taking the risk. If this rumor proves false, "

"I doubt it," Barro cut in gruffly. "Too many coincidences point to someone within our ranks. And the watchtower's been a known blind spot for too long." His gaze slanted to Taron. "Are you certain you want to confront him yourself, my lord? It could provoke...unwanted side effects."

A muscle in Taron's jaw flexed, the only sign of his frustration. "I have to," he said. "If a knight of our own is feeding sabotage details to the Baron Felstain, I can't stand idle. I won't let Cassandra face him alone."

Cassandra's chest warmed briefly at his words, a traitorous flicker of gratitude. She still wrestled with old resentments, but in these moments, when Taron chose to stand by her, risking himself, she couldn't deny the surge of affection and concern that rose within her. Schooling her features, she pinned Sir Barro with a determined look. "Lead the way. Quietly, if we can."

He nodded curtly, angling his helmet over his head once more. Then he guided them across the empty courtyard. They skirted along the perimeter, using the shadows cast by tall battlements to remain unseen. A single guard patrolled the upper wall, but if Sir Barro's efforts kept him busy, they wouldn't have to explain why Taron and Cassandra were sneaking to the watchtower so late.

The ancient stones of the rampart staircase felt chilled beneath Cassandra's palm as they ascended. Far below, the courtyard seemed to shrink into a patchwork of stone. She caught sight of only one faint torch glimmering by the stable yard. Everything else lay hushed. Each breath she took felt louder than it should, echoing in her ears.

They reached a narrow walkway near the top of the outer wall. From there, a short spur of masonry led toward the watchtower's side entrance. An arch separated the tower from the main keep, presumably once used by archers to patrol. Sir Barro motioned for caution, pressing a gloved finger to his lips.

Cassandra nodded. She opened her senses, seeking the subtle prickle of runic energy that might betray hidden traps. At first, she felt nothing but the normal background hum of Taron's aura. Then she caught a faint tingle in the stone beneath her boots: a sign that runic devices were close by. Not quite wards, something sharper, more predatory. Her chest tightened.

She found Taron's gaze in the gloom, noting how his eyes glowed faintly. It was the telltale sign of his magic stirring in response to nearby interference. The very air seemed to hush around him.

"Wait," Cassandra whispered, laying her hand on Sir Barro's arm. "I feel something."

Barro froze. Taron tensed, stepping nearer. He inhaled in that way he did when bracing for an unwelcome wave of power. "Devices?" he asked under his breath.

Cassandra swallowed. "Likely. If the saboteur, this knight, has a stash of runic triggers, we need to move carefully. I can place a small ward around us, just in case we cross any magical trip line."

Cassandra pulled a slender piece of chalk from her pouch. She knelt on the cold, worn stones of the walkway, the chalk trembling slightly in her fingers as she began to draw. The air felt alive, charged with an almost imperceptible hum of predatory energy, and she knew they were walking a razor-thin line.

Sir Barro watched her with silent respect. Once, he would have eyed her chalk as if it were poison, but now, after all the crises she'd averted, he seemed quietly grateful for her skill.

If she made a mistake, if the saboteur's traps were tripped, the consequences would be swift and catastrophic. She swallowed hard, her focus sharpening as the runes began to take shape beneath her hand. Each stroke had to be precise—no margin for error.

She started with the outer circle, a smooth, unbroken line that shimmered faintly in the moonlight. Inside, she carved symbols for protection and containment: an angular ward to absorb external forces, a looping sigil to dampen volatile magic. Her movements were methodical, practiced, though tension gripped her shoulders as she worked. Taron and Sir Barro stood close, their breaths hushed, their gazes flickering between her and the shadowed tower ahead.

"Stand within the circle," she said, her voice steady despite the thrum of nerves in her chest. "Don't step outside of it, no matter what you feel. This ward will contain most magical interference, but only if we remain inside its boundaries."

They both obeyed, no questions asked. stepped in immediately, his boots scuffing softly on the stone as he moved into the circle's center. His eyes, still faintly glowing from the lingering stir of his aura, met hers. "What about you?" he asked, his voice low but firm.

"I'll be inside the circle when I finish the sigils," she replied, her tone leaving no room for argument. "Don't worry. This isn't the first time I've worked against hostile wards."

Still, his jaw tightened, and the faint twitch in his hands betrayed his anxiety. Cassandra refused to let it distract her. She finished the final sigil—a spiraling glyph meant to neutralize sudden bursts of magic—then stepped inside the circle, and placed her palm flat in the circle's center, right next to where Taron stood. The runes glowed brighter, faint lines of gold spreading outward like veins across the stone.

She closed her eyes, letting her breathing steady. "Circulus et amplexus," she intoned softly, her voice carrying an ancient rhythm. "Protect those within my sight. Bind the unseen, tame the storm."

She felt the energy stir beneath her hand, a pulse of warmth that traveled through her arm like liquid fire. The circle began to hum, the faint glow of the runes intensifying as they linked together. "Through earth and sky, I anchor the chaos. By will and purpose, I seal this space. Nox et lux, unum fiat."

The air within the circle grew heavy, charged with tangible pressure. Cassandra opened her eyes, watching as the runes flickered once, twice, and then steadied into a soft, golden glow. The ward was active, a fragile but resilient shield against the saboteur's traps.

Taron's gaze hadn't left her, and his voice cut through the charged silence. "What if their traps are layered? Will this hold?"

She exhaled, brushing chalk dust from her fingers as she stood. "It'll hold long enough for us to assess what we're dealing with. If something activates, the ward will buy us seconds to react. But we need to move carefully." She looked at Sir Barro, who gave her a terse nod, his expression grim but trusting.

As they turned their attention back to the looming tower, Cassandra stepped closer to Taron, her voice dropping to a whisper. "Stay within the lines, no matter what. If the traps are designed to target your aura, stepping outside could trigger them."

He nodded, his expression hardening with determination. "I'll stay close. But if something goes wrong..." His hand brushed hers briefly, a fleeting touch that sent a spark of warmth through her amidst the tension. "You step back. Promise me."

Her lips curved faintly, though the weight of their situation pressed heavily on her. "Let's just make sure it doesn't come to that." She turned her focus forward, the golden glow of the ward casting faint light across the stones as they moved toward the tower, every step measured, every breath a calculated risk. "I think it's safe to move now. I guess we'll see if the ritual works or not as we approach the watchtower."

THEY CREPT SLOWLY ONWARD. The watchtower loomed overhead, spindly vines creeping up its weathered stone. A narrow door, half-rotted, stood ajar. Through the gap, a thread of light flickered. Cassandra tensed, exchanging a glance with Taron. Someone was definitely inside.

Sir Barro leaned in. "We should see if we can overhear anything," he murmured. "Then decide whether to confront him or wait for my men to flank the tower."

Taron nodded, but a faint hum buzzed in the air, like a static charge that made the hair on Cassandra's arms lift. She recognized it from the farmland sabotage: the ominous resonance of runic tools designed to draw forth Taron's power. Fear jolted her pulse. If the saboteur used such a device in these cramped quarters, Taron might be forced into a meltdown with nowhere to dissipate the energy except straight into the walls, and the people inside.

"I don't think we have time to wait," she whispered, heart thumping. "We need to move before they can fully activate whatever that is."

Taron's expression flashed with grim agreement. Sir

Barro gave a curt nod, hand poised on his sword hilt. Then, together, they pressed closer to the door.

A low murmur of voices drifted out. Cassandra strained to catch the words, but they were scattered and hushed, "...deliveries tomorrow... sabotage... worthless witch..." Her teeth ground at the mention of "witch," though she steeled herself, focusing on the immediate threat.

Sir Barro signaled for Taron and Cassandra to position themselves on either side of the door. Then, in one fluid motion, he kicked it open. The door crashed inward, sending splinters of rotten wood across a dusty stone floor. Torchlight streaked the darkness.

TWENTY-SEVEN

Three figures whipped around. One was indeed a knight in battered armor bearing Ulric's crest, though his face was half-hidden by a ragged hood. The other two wore dark leathers. Mercenaries, Cassandra realized, heart stuttering. Their startled curses broke the silence.

"Stop!" Sir Barro commanded, blade glinting. "Drop your weapons!"

For a heartbeat, the conspirators froze. Cassandra recognized one of their own knights among the saboteurs: Sir Brieland. Was he working for the rival? Was he the turncoat?

Sir Brieland lurched backward, hand diving into a satchel slung across his shoulder. Cassandra caught a glimpse of something sinisterly etched: a runic device glimmering with swirling lines. Her pulse leaped.

"Taron, watch out!" she cried.

But it was too late. One of the mercenaries yanked out

a second device, twisting a small dial that flared bright with runic light. Immediately, Cassandra felt the energy shift, a tidal wave latching onto Taron's aura. The air thickened, crackling as if struck by sudden lightning.

Taron let out a ragged gasp, staggering. "They're trying...to pull," His words choked off, eyes widening with alarm. Wisps of silver-blue light glowed at the edges of his gloved hands. The sabotage runes from the farmland fiasco had done the same. Cassandra recognized the trap: forcibly drawing Taron's magic outward to destabilize him.

Her mind raced. If Taron's magic surged in here, the tight corridor would become a blast furnace. She seized a chunk of chalk, dropping to one knee and inscribing a hasty ward circle on the tower's floor. It wasn't as strong as she'd like, there wasn't time. She pressed her palm to the half-formed circle, channeling a shock of her magic into it.

A shimmering barrier materialized around Taron, faint and wavering. She felt the jabbing pressure of that runic device straining to break through. Her hands trembled as she poured more of her energy in. "Give me a moment!" she hissed to Sir Barro, who had lunged forward to engage the mercenaries.

Chaos broke out. Swords clanged, steel on steel. Sir Brieland swung his blade at Sir Barro, who parried with a grunt. One of the mercenaries tried to flank them, but Taron, fighting for breath, still managed to pivot and fling up an arm. An arc of his barely contained magic deflected the mercenary's rush, hurling the man back into a rickety crate. It collapsed with a tremendous crash.

Cassandra's ward flickered. She clenched her jaw, drawing a deeper thread of power from within. A line of sweat trickled down her temple. "Taron don't fight it alone," she urged through gritted teeth. "Let me anchor you."

He exhaled shakily, nodding as he locked his gaze on her. Even from a few paces away, she could feel the magnetism of his aura, the sizzling tension that threatened to devour him. His voice came out shaky: "I... I'm trying."

The device in the mercenary's grasp pulsed. Cassandra's eyes flicked to it, noticing an eerie pattern of runes swirling. She recognized the design from half-finished sketches in the sabotage logs: lethal contraptions meant to induce meltdown. If she didn't sever that link, Taron would erupt like a volcano.

Gripping her chalk, she crawled closer, maintaining the ward around Taron as best she could. The magical strain weighed on her like iron chains. Her breath grew labored, but she forced herself onward. The mercenary was pinned under the collapsed crate, fumbling to free himself. Cassandra saw an opening: a moment to tear the device from his hands before he could fully activate it.

Cassandra's eyes caught the glint of something etched with swirling lines of energy, a runic device glowing with an ominous, unearthly light. Her pulse leaped.

"Runes!" she shouted, her voice cutting through the charged air. "He's activating something—"

But Taron was already moving. His hand shot out, and with a roar of raw power, his aura erupted around him, a storm of electric-blue light swirling like a living force. The sheer pressure of it sent a shockwave rippling across the room, rattling the loose stones of the watchtower. Brieland stumbled, but his fingers clawed for the device, yanking it free.

"Don't let him activate it!" Cassandra cried, scrambling toward Brieland. With a sweep of her hand, she hurled a hastily drawn warding line toward him, the chalk in her palm sparking with her energy. The line flared, searing through the air like a whip, striking Brieland's arm. He hissed in pain, dropping the device—but not before it emitted a burst of violent red light.

The room erupted into chaos. Another conspirator, a wiry man with a blade in hand, lunged toward Taron, aiming for his unguarded side. Taron spun, the glow of his aura intensifying as he raised his arm. The blade never connected; the energy field surrounding him expanded, a shield of sheer force that sent the attacker skidding backward. The man hit the wall with a sickening thud and slumped to the floor, groaning.

Cassandra darted toward the fallen device, but Brieland wasn't finished. He snarled, pulling a second rune-laden object from his satchel—a small orb crackling with unstable energy. He slammed it against the ground, and an eruption of fiery sparks shot outward, the force nearly knocking her off her feet. Heat seared the air, and Cassandra threw up her arms as her protective ward absorbed most of the blast. Even so, the impact sent her stumbling back.

"Cassandra!" Taron's voice was a growl, vibrating with the intensity of his magic. His aura flared brighter, crackling around him in tendrils of light that scorched the floor where he stood. He surged forward, one hand raised, and a jagged arc of energy shot from his palm. It struck Brieland's chest like a bolt of lightning, sending the man reeling with a scream of pain. The satchel fell from his shoulder, scattering its contents —runes, scrolls, and a third device that pulsed dangerously.

"Get those runes!" Taron barked, his voice was like thunder.

Cassandra didn't hesitate. She dove for the satchel, her fingers curling around the edge just as another conspirator lunged for her. She rolled to the side, narrowly avoiding the dagger aimed for her back, and kicked out with her heel. The blow connected with the man's knee, and he crumpled with a grunt of pain. Rising quickly, she grabbed the scattered runes and shoved them into her pouch, her heart pounding as she worked to gather them before another explosion could be triggered.

Brieland, however, wasn't finished. He staggered to his feet, clutching his chest where Taron's magic had struck. His eyes burned with fury, and he began chanting under his breath, his voice laced with venomous intent. The runes etched into his armor began to glow, and Cassandra realized with horror that he was pulling in energy from the surrounding room. The very air seemed to warp and ripple around him.

"Taron, he's drawing power—stop him!" she yelled, her voice breaking with urgency.

Taron didn't need the warning. He stepped forward, the glow of his aura intensifying until it was nearly blinding. His hands lifted, palms outstretched, and a vortex of energy spiraled outward, colliding with the force Brieland had conjured. The two opposing powers met in a violent clash, the resulting shockwave shaking the tower to its foundation. Stones cracked and dust rained from the ceiling as the forces pushed against each other, neither giving an inch.

Cassandra felt the heat of the clash as she scrambled back, her wards flaring to life around her in a protective shield. She watched as Taron advanced step by step, his power driving Brieland's energy backward. The conspirator's face twisted with effort, veins standing out on his neck as he tried to hold his ground. But Taron's magic was relentless, fueled by fury and the unshakable resolve in his eyes.

Sir Barro was locked in a precarious duel with Brieland's knights, their swords clashing. Another mercenary lunged at Taron from behind, brandishing a short-bladed weapon that flickered with its own runic lines. Cassandra shouted a warning, but her voice was drowned in the echoes of steel and the roar of Taron's magic surging.

He spun, just in time, raising a trembling hand that crackled with arcane light. The mercenary's blade slammed into a veil of that shimmering force. Sparks spat in all directions. Taron gasped, pushing the attacker back a step. But the flicker in Taron's aura told Cassandra the effort cost him heavily. She sensed his control slipping.

She refused to let him go under. Grunting, she forced her ward to expand. The ephemeral circle pulsed outward, encasing Taron in a faint glow that halted the mercenary's second strike. But beneath that glow, Cassandra felt Taron's panic. Her own heart thundered. If they didn't neutralize those devices, he'd be a blazing torch.

From the corner of her eye, she glimpsed the pinned mercenary raising the dial again, a desperate attempt to intensify the runic pull. Cassandra lurched forward. Her ward around Taron wobbled, but she seized the man's wrist before he could turn the dial. He snarled, eyes wide with fear or fury.

"Not tonight," Cassandra spat, tightening her grip. She poured a sliver of her magic down her arm, letting it spark at her fingertips. Her grandmother's ring, no, she reminded herself, she wore no ring but had the memory of her mentor's words that she could sharpen her healing energy into a protective jolt. She released just enough to shock the mercenary's muscles into a brief spasm.

He yowled and dropped the device. Cassandra snatched it, ignoring the sting as runic arcs licked at her knuckles. She flung it away across the tower floor. It skittered and banged against a low stone wall. The glow dimmed. Immediately, she felt a lessening of the strangling effect on Taron. Not gone, but less intense.

Meanwhile, Taron deflected another slash from the armed mercenary. The man's strike glanced off a swirl of Taron's newfound arcane shield. Sparks flew close enough to singe Taron's sleeve, but he held firm. Cassandra's ward was still clinging to him, battered but functional.

Sir Barro slammed Sir Brieland's weapon aside with a fierce blow. The knight stumbled, breathing heavily, eyes wild. The battered hood slipped back, revealing sallow cheeks and a twisted sneer.

He bared his teeth. "Fools," he spat. "You can't protect him forever, he'll destroy everything. And she's the real threat," he snarled, glaring at Cassandra with naked hatred. "The saboteur is the witch, not me."

"Give it a rest," Sir Barro snapped, pressing the advantage. Though the knight was cunning, Barro's skill was steadier. Their swords crashed into a flurry of sparks.

Cassandra's lungs burned, but she scrambled to her feet, scanning for any other devices. She spotted a small pack on the table near the tower's far side. A flicker of runic light glowed from within. Another sabotage tool. She cursed under her breath and wove toward it, desperately clinging to the mental threads of Taron's ward. The double effort, sustaining the magical shield and searching for the next device, tugged at her, threatening to split her focus.

Behind her, Taron groaned. She risked a glance over her shoulder. The second mercenary hammered at him again, the runic blade crackling with a sickly green edge. Taron's shield fed off Cassandra's energy as well as his own. If she left it for too long, he would stand unprotected against a lethal blow.

A flash of guilt and fear spurred her to quicken her pace. If she could just destroy that other device...

She reached the table and flung aside a battered ledger. Underneath lay a lump-shaped bag with luminous runes etched around the opening. She didn't recognize the exact pattern, but everything in her gut screamed it was trouble. Where in the realms had they gotten so many dangerous runic contraptions?

She grabbed the bag, half-expecting it to burn her. The runes hissed on contact, arcs of pale green dancing across her knuckles. Cassandra bit back a cry, forcing her magic outward, hoping to disrupt the design. She used the side of a small dagger from her belt to cut the cord, severing the runes' continuity. The glow sputtered out like a candle snuffed by wind.

Before she could breathe relief, a searing pulse of magic cut the air. Taron's voice tore in a hoarse cry. Cassandra whirled, heart in her throat.

The second mercenary had cornered Taron against the wall. Taron's aura flared, scattering broken planks and stone dust. The backlash from his surge threatened to blow them all to bits. Cassandra felt the last threads of her ward around him unravel the tension snapping in her mind.

No, she couldn't let him meltdown. She dashed forward, ignoring the leftover sting in her arm from the sabotage runes. Silver light flared from Taron's fingertips, wild arcs coiling around his body in chaotic bursts. The mercenary was knocked back, momentarily stunned, but Taron was losing control. She could see it in his eyes, wide, full of horror that he might unleash something irreversible.

TWENTY-EIGHT

"Cassandra!" he managed, voice tight with desperation.

She skidded to a stop at his side, pressing her palm against his chest. The heat of his magic jolted her; it was nearly scalding through his tunic. She inhaled, focusing on grounding him again. Though battered from the scuffle, she forced calm into her voice. "Look at me," she said, lifting her other hand to brush across his jaw. "Focus on my wards. We channel this together."

He closed his eyes, breath shuddering. She felt the raw wave of energy roiling inside him. Gritting her teeth, she visualized the protective wards she'd studied so many times, the careful geometry that siphoned excess power without harming the caster. That was the delicate symmetry that stabilized Taron's aura.

With trembling concentration, she laced her magic into his. It felt like trying to contain an earthquake in a jar, every muscle in her body shook with the strain. The air around them swirled in bright motes of silver and gold, the combined hue of their power brushing the tower walls. Outside, she heard Sir Barro's blade clash with the turncoat's again, but everything else faded into the roar of Taron's surge.

Gradually, agonizingly, the chaos receded. The arcs around Taron dimmed from a raging firestorm to a flicker of lightning. Cassandra kept her hands on him, ignoring her own ragged breathing, ignoring the swirl of dust that stung her eyes. She would not relent until she was sure he was stable.

He finally eased out his breath. "I, I'm good," he whispered hoarsely. Then his knees buckled, and she caught him, her arms hooking around his waist.

Before she could say more, a feral shout erupted across the room. "You worthless scum!" Sir Brieland, having briefly disengaged from Sir Barro, now brandished a short crossbow loaded with a bolt that glowed faint green, a runic tip. He leveled it at Taron's exposed flank.

Fear stabbed Cassandra. She had no time to weave a new shield. Taron, half-collapsed in her arms, was in no position to dodge. She lunged, twisting her body to shield him. But the whistle of steel cut the air, a blur of motion that revealed Sir Barro tackling the knight from behind. The bolt clattered harmlessly against the flagstones, bouncing away with a sharp clang. Cassandra's heart pounded.

"Stay down!" Barro growled. He slammed the man's head into the stone floor, disarming him of the crossbow.

The knight spat curses, thrashing. But Barro's hold was unyielding.

That left one mercenary accounted for, but where was the other? Cassandra's attention snapped to the side. The pinned mercenary she had shocked was gone, only an overturned crate remained. Her pulse hammered. The watchtower's narrow interior was wreathed in dust and chaotic darkness, so it was possible the mercenary had slipped out through a side door or crack in the wall.

"Taron," Cassandra murmured, "can you stand?"

He nodded weakly, leaning heavily on her. "I'll manage."

"Then we,"

She broke off at a sudden hiss. Smoke began to fill the tower, curling from somewhere near the far side. A rancid scent bit her nostrils, thick, acrid. Some kind of smoke bomb, possibly from the missing mercenary. A swirl of gray vapor expanded, stinging Cassandra's eyes and making her cough.

Sir Barro jerked up, eyes flicking around in alarm. "They're covering their escape." Indeed, footsteps pounded near the back corner. Another wooden door she hadn't noticed gave a hollow creak. The second mercenary must have triggered the bomb and fled.

Cassandra gritted her teeth, trying to blink away the haze. She heard more footsteps outside, possibly Barro's men rushing to intercept. But the watchtower was rapidly filling with noxious smoke. Taron's ragged breathing turned harsh in her ear.

"Come on," she urged, grasping his arm. She barely saw Barro coughing as he yanked Sir Brieland to his feet in a rough hold. They staggered together toward the half-smashed door where they'd entered.

A distant clang from the courtyard indicated some scuffle. The wind from outside offered a mercy of fresh air as they stumbled onto the rampart walkway. Cassandra's eyes watered uncontrollably; her throat raw from the smoke. Taron clutched at the stone wall for support, still trembling in the aftermath of his surge.

Sir Barro dragged the captive knight along, the man's hood half torn away to reveal sweat-streaked hair and a contorted expression of hatred. "Let me go!" he spat, but Barro only tightened his grip. A smear of blood trickled from the knight's temple.

A few of Barro's men sprinted up the walkway from the courtyard side, swords drawn. "Sir! The mercenaries, some fled the tower's back exit," one reported breathlessly. "We tried to cut them off, but they vanished into a bolt-hole near the base. Looks like a tunnel that leads outside the keep's perimeter."

Cassandra's heart sank. So, they had an escape route planned all along. She coughed, pressing her hand to her chest. Through bleary eyes, she saw Taron leaning heavily against the stone parapet, face pale. Despite that, he glanced around in alarm. "Tools... they had too many runic tools," he managed between coughs. "They know exactly how to twist my surges."

Sir Barro looked grave. He snapped at his men, "Take

him", he shook the captive knight, "to the guardhouse. Lock him down tight. I'll interrogate him once we secure the area." The knight struggled, but two other knights stepped in and hauled him away.

A hush fell among the remaining men. They studied Taron and Cassandra with anxious expressions. The ring of sabotage extended even within the keep, and now the conspirators had shown they had an entire arsenal of runic devices, not just a scattered few.

Seeing the tension, Cassandra steadied herself. Her limbs felt shaky from channeling so much magic, but she forced her spine straight and turned to Taron. "Are you all right?" The question came out ragged.

He blinked, forcing a shallow nod. "I'll survive. Thanks to you. But we almost," His gaze flickered to the tower, still emitting wisps of foul-smelling smoke. He swallowed. "They were seconds away from forcing me into a meltdown that might've collapsed half this place."

She grabbed his hand, not caring who witnessed. The memory of that savage tug on his aura made her skin crawl. "We need to stop them from ever trying that again," she whispered.

He squeezed her fingers, eyes searching hers. "We will," he vowed, voice thick with anger and leftover tremors. "I'm done letting them use my power as a weapon."

Sir Barro cleared his throat, stepping closer once he'd sent the others away with instructions to comb the tower for any missed contraband. "We have a partial victory," he said quietly. "We captured the renegade knight and at least some of the sabotage runes. That will help confirm your innocence, Cassandra. But the larger threat remains at large." His normally stoic face was grim. "It's obvious this is bigger than one turncoat. These mercenaries are well-provisioned, and they know exactly how to exploit Taron's weak points."

Cassandra's stomach churned. She thought of the farmland fiasco, the tampered warding posts, the letter referencing Black Sigils. The infiltration ran deeper than they'd feared. "They must be in league with...someone powerful," she said, glancing at Taron. "A Baron Felstain who stands to gain from sowing chaos here, or at least from making you seem too dangerous to rule."

Even in the gloom, she read the flicker of agreement in Taron's exhausted eyes. "We can't keep letting them corner us in secret corners of the keep," he said. "They slip away every time. We need to get more information from the renegade. Ensure he's not put to death."

Sir Barro nodded. "I'll double the watch on every corridor, every entry point that's not sealed. We'll dispatch men to block that bolt-hole if possible. But there may be other routes yet unknown."

Cassandra pressed her lips into a thin line. Something inside her tensed at the realization: if the saboteur's network had studied Taron's wards so closely, they might have also charted every hidden passage in the keep. She recalled the day she discovered runes scrawled in the farmland posts, all designed to siphon Taron's aura. These conspirators were cunning, systematic. Staking out the watchtower was just one piece of their plan.

She tugged Taron's arm gently, encouraging him to step away from the tower's outer walkway. The night air was brisk, and she could see him shiver, whether from cold or lingering shock. Despite everything, a surge of tenderness rose in her chest, an impulse to protect him. It startled her how much she cared for him, even after all the heartbreak. But now was not the time to puzzle over her own feelings; the threat demanded relentless focus.

"We should get back, regroup," she said. "We can't linger out here in case some other ambush is waiting. And Taron needs rest, or he won't be able to fend off another surge."

He opened his mouth as if to protest, but exhaustion and pain ghosted across his features. "Cassandra's right," Sir Barro said firmly. "Return to your chambers. My men will escort you. I'll handle the prisoner and secure more guards."

Taron nodded reluctantly. "Very well." Then, quieter, he glanced at Cassandra. "I don't want to leave you alone in this, though."

She managed a small, grim smile. "You won't. But first, you need to recover enough to keep us both safe next time."

His throat bobbed, eyes meeting hers in a moment of unspoken intimacy. She thought she heard the faintest catch in his breath. The courtyard's murky gloom and the swirl of moonlight brushed his face in a soft glow that highlighted the conflict in his gaze: gratitude, fury at the saboteurs, and a deeper worry that he might still fail her. She squeezed his hand, letting him feel her conviction.

Sir Barro signaled a pair of knights to form a protective circle around Taron and Cassandra as they made their way back down the walkway. Below, the courtyard stretched in shadowed emptiness, only a few torches illuminating the main gate. Flickers of movement near the guardhouse told her the captive was being dragged inside. A pang of relief that at least one conspirator wouldn't vanish into the night with the others.

Their descent was slow; Taron's breath rasped, and Cassandra could almost taste the lingering tang of ozone from his near-surge. She walked close beside him, not quite touching but ready to lend support if he collapsed. Every step reminded her how close it had been, one flick of that runic dial separating them from a catastrophic meltdown. The saboteur's malice had grown bolder, more dangerous.

At the bottom of the staircase, they paused in a narrow passage between two walls. The sky overhead revealed a slice of moon. She took the last steps with Taron's elbow lightly brushing her side, an unspoken reassurance that neither of them was alone. Sir Barro, a pace ahead, halted, glancing back with a measured look.

"We've confirmed they escaped," he said tightly. "At least two of them are gone, plus that turned knight's allies. The tower's entrance was rigged with that smoke for a swift getaway." His mouth thinned. "They'll likely regroup. If this was an ambush to kill or coerce Taron, it almost succeeded."

Taron's hand curled into a fist. "But they failed." There was an edge of defiance in his voice beneath the worn exhaustion.

Cassandra released a shaky breath. "Yes, they did. And we've gleaned something valuable: they rely on these runic weapons to trigger your surges. That means if we can strip them of those devices, or sabotage them back, we can level the field." Her mind raced with the possibilities. Studying the confiscated runes might reveal how to break their effect on Taron permanently.

Sir Barro grunted in agreement. "I'll see to it the devices are collected, locked down. If you can investigate them safely, do so. But we should hurry back. The courtyard's not secure."

The knights guided them onward, crossing the courtyard properly. Night's chill nipped at Cassandra's cloak. The keep's walls, high and imposing, felt even more shadowed than usual. Each corner or arch seemed to lurk with unspoken threats. She forced her shoulders not to hunch, determined not to show how rattled she was.

Soon, they neared the broad doors that led into the main corridor of the keep. Light from two wall-mounted torches flickered across Taron's face, showing lines of fatigue. He leaned close enough that she heard the raggedness in his breathing. Yet he met her gaze and managed a faint, reassuring nod.

Inside, the corridor was dim, the sconces half-burned out. The small escort parted ways, two knights accompanied Sir Barro to secure the watchtower's prisoner, while another pair stuck to Cassandra and Taron. Their footsteps echoed. She wondered how many staff or lesser knights they passed who might have glimpsed Taron's battered form, her sooty cloak, and guessed that another meltdown had nearly occurred tonight. Rumors would swirl by sunrise.

CHAPTER

TWENTY-NINE

Eventually, they reached the corridor that branched off toward Taron's chamber and Cassandra's modest quarters. The knights peered around warily. No immediate danger presented itself. One knight hesitated, obviously assigned to "watch" Cassandra per some directive from Baron Ulric, but Taron spoke up:

"Leave us for a moment." Though fatigue laced his tone, a quiet command underpinned it. "We'll be safe in this corridor. I want to speak with Cassandra alone."

The knights exchanged glances. One gave a curt nod. "Very well, my lord. We'll remain just around the corner if you need assistance."

Their footsteps receded, leaving only the shuffle of Taron's breath and the distant flicker of a mounted lamp. Cassandra turned, heart pounding unexpectedly. The corridor felt too quiet, walls echoing tension.

Taron slid a hand across the stone wall to steady himself. Without the protective ring of guards, she saw how truly exhausted he was, shoulders drooping beneath the weight of spent magic. Concern flared, unbidden. Placing her hand lightly on his forearm, she said, "Sit, before you collapse."

He gave a weary chuckle, sliding down to sit on the corridor's step. She sank beside him, the cold stone leaching warmth through her cloak. The hush between them thrummed with unsaid confessions. After a second, he raised his head, meeting her eyes.

"That was too close," he said softly. "Every time I think we've accounted for their sabotage; they show a new way to force my aura out of control."

She exhaled, feeling the aftershocks of tension coil in her gut. "We'll find a way to stop them," she murmured. "Tonight, we seized at least one conspirator and some of their runic weapons. We'll learn something from that. And you, " She gentled her tone, caution in her expression. "You need rest, Taron. Each meltdown takes its toll."

He let out a hollow laugh. "Rest? Right. With mercenaries and rogue knights turning the keep into a trap? With my father still threatening you unless I demonstrate I can 'control' my magic?" His voice caught on the final word.

Her chest twisted. She recalled the farmland sabotage, how the baron used each incident to paint her as incompetent. Now, the conspirators had proven they could strike in the heart of the fortress. She put a hand on Taron's knee, an unplanned gesture of quiet solidarity. "I'm not leaving," she whispered. "Not until this is over."

A flicker of relief crossed his face. Then something else,

an ache. "You could have died in there," he said. "They nearly aimed that runic blade at your back. I saw it, and I," He cut himself short. Without thinking, he reached up, brushed a strand of her hair away from her cheek. The faint touch sent a ripple of warmth through her.

Her voice trembled with sincerity she couldn't quite hide. "I knew the risk. Nothing matters more than stopping them from twisting your magic."

His eyes closed for a moment; a line etched between his brows. "Cassandra...I'm sorry you have to bear this." Then, quieter, "I hate having to rely on you to keep me stable, but I...I'm also grateful. Because I trust you more than I trust anyone."

Emotion clutched at her. She remembered all the times she'd resented him for not defending her. But on nights like this, they stood side by side against shadows, forging a connection that had only grown stronger under siege. She inhaled shakily. "Then trust me when I say we can't face them alone. Sir Barro's men are loyal, but we need more than force. We need knowledge, how they keep creating or procuring these runic triggers. If it's truly a Baron Felstain behind them, we must gather proof."

"I know," he murmured, leaning his head back against the wall. "Tonight was a start. But the real battle is still ahead."

She clasped her hands in her lap, resisting the urge to smooth a thumb over his temple. "We'll notify the keep at once, like we planned," she said. "Have Sir Barro station more guards, secure every approach. Then we'll examine those devices, see if we can neutralize them or trace them.

And if another ambush hits," She paused, letting the promise settle. "We'll be ready."

He nodded, opening his mouth to respond. But a wave of exhaustion seemed to steal his words. In the silence, Cassandra felt the faint brush of his hand near hers, the slightest shift that let their fingers graze. She might have drawn back, uncertain, but for once, she didn't. She let the fleeting contact remain, a fragile tether binding them in this empty corridor.

Minutes ticked by their hearts pounding in unison. Outside, the keep loomed with hidden threats, and the conspirators who escaped would surely plan another attempt. Yet for this sliver of time, she let the hush envelop them. The stone's chill seeped through her clothes, but Taron's magic, the calmer undercurrent, still thrummed in her awareness, comforting in its warmth.

At last, she broke the hush. "We should go," she murmured. "Before the knights worry."

He inhaled, lifting his head. "Yes." Then he managed to make a small, weary smile. "Though it's tempting just to... stay here for a moment longer."

His wry admission coaxed a faint smile from her as well, the tension in her chest loosening for the briefest instant. In that shared look, she saw recognition of everything they'd endured. They both rose, leaning on each other for balance as they trudged down the corridor. The knights stepped forward at once, relieved to see Taron still upright.

"Return him to his chamber," Cassandra said quietly to the guards. "Ensure he's not disturbed by anyone except Sir Barro or me." She didn't have the baron's official authority, but something in her tone brooked no argument. They snapped to attention, offering Taron a respectful nod. Once, they might have questioned deferring to a witch. Not anymore.

Taron's gaze lingered on her. "And you?" he asked, voice low.

She pressed a hand to the wall, steadied by the rough texture. "I'll go to my room...but not for long. Barro needs me to identify those runic devices we confiscated." A pang of worry flickered. "We have to move quickly, Taron."

He inclined his head in silent agreement. Then, with a final, meaningful look, he allowed the knights to guide him away. Cassandra watched him vanish around a bend in the corridor, the tension in her gut refusing to dissolve. The exchange in the watchtower weighed on her, the near-catastrophe one more step in a deadly dance orchestrated by unseen conspirators.

When she turned down a side corridor, the flicker of candlelight caught on a dusty tapestry, reminding her that this keep held centuries of secrets. She drew a shaky breath, forcing her mind to sharpen. Their foes were bold enough to brandish runic devices in the very heart of the castle. She and Taron had survived only by a razor-thin margin.

But they survived. And they had a prisoner, one piece of the hidden plot. She clung to that victory, however fragile, as she made her way toward her chamber. Sir Barro would meet her soon to discuss the next steps. Together, they'd pry answers out of that Sir Brieland, discover how the mercenaries had gotten so many dangerous runes, and close the bolt-hole path if at all possible. And she would find a way to fortify Taron's wards so that no sabotage could claw at his magic again.

Her thoughts spun with plans and half-formed strategies, but the deeper thread was pure resolve. Tonight had proven that the saboteur's net ran wide, and that Taron's aura remained the perfect target for a forced meltdown. But with each passing confrontation, Cassandra and Taron's combined magic grew steadier, each conflict forging trust in the midst of uncertainty.

She reached her chamber door. Two weary guards stationed outside stepped aside to let her in, giving her guarded nods. Inside, the small room felt closer than ever, the air was thick with the smell of extinguished candles and her tension-laced sweat. She eased the door shut, leaning her forehead against the wood for an instant, letting out a ragged sigh. Her limbs trembled from exhaustion and leftover adrenaline.

Closing her eyes, she recalled the moment Taron's magic flared in the watchtower, how close it had come to destroying them both. And how, pressed against the cold masonry, they'd steadied each other, hearts hammering in unison. That memory sent a wisp of heat through her chest, equal parts relief and something else she couldn't name.

Then she turned away from the door, forcing her chin up. The night was far from over, but she'd keep fighting until the saboteur's stranglehold was broken for good. They might come again, bombarding Taron's aura with new runic horrors. But if they did, she'd be ready, because for all her lingering resentments, she refused to let them break Taron or the barony. Not while she had breath left in her body.

Her pulse steadied. Even if the conspirators struck on another midnight, like prowling wolves, Cassandra and Taron would not be cornered so easily again. Tightening her fists, she crossed the room to gather a fresh piece of chalk and the battered notes on sabotage runes she'd begun compiling. The watchtower confrontation had nearly ended in disaster, but it had also galvanized her. She would unravel each new threat, protect Taron from their cunning weapons, and see this through to the end.

Whatever the conspirators planned next, whatever dark sabotage might lurk in the shadows, she and Taron would stand together. And for the first time since her return, Cassandra let a flicker of genuine hope spark to life. The barony was under siege from within, but they were no longer blind to it. Holding tight to that conviction, she braced herself for what was sure to be another long night.

CHAPTER

THIRTY

Dawn broke in a pale haze of gold and gray, spilling across the castle's courtyard and climbing the stone walls like tentative fingers. Cassandra stood near the frost-dusted windows of her cramped chamber, arms crossed around herself, heart pounding faster with every distant murmur that reached her through the corridors. She could sense tension gathering throughout Baron Ulric's keep, taut and dangerous. Rumors crackled in the torchlit hallways, stretching from the guard towers to the servants' passages, all echoing the same cry: that Taron's surging magic risked upending them all.

She inhaled shakily, trying to keep her composure. Her breath emerged in unsteady puffs against the window's chill. Though the keep had never felt particularly safe for her, it felt doubly hostile this morning. The events of the previous night were still fresh in her mind, secret ambushes, sabotage, Taron's near-loss of control. Worse, that hooded figure in the library who had stolen a hidden parchment. Every sign pointed to infiltration. Yet from the sounds drifting up from below, Baron Ulric would twist that fear into a fresh assault against her. Or perhaps he would further corner Taron, forcing him into some new directive that served the baron's power.

She clenched her fists. Suppose she had a choice, she could bolt and vanish into the forest, leaving Taron to wrestle with his father's demands alone. It would be safer for her own life. But each time that thought rose, a memory flashed of Taron's pained expression, of how he clung to her presence to anchor his magic. She could not abandon him to the conspirators who'd unleash a meltdown. Perhaps deeper still, she would not abandon him, for reasons that made her heart twist.

A rap on her door startled her. She recognized the brisk pattern, one of the keep's stewards, perhaps. Cassandra braced herself and swung the door open. Indeed, a steward in a dark doublet stood there, face pale with tension.

"Lady Cassandra," he said, his tone half-hushed. "The baron... The baron demands you join the council at once."

Her stomach clenched uneasily at the formality. "Why now?"

"When you arrive, you shall see," he replied, eyes flicking aside. Then, in a quieter voice, "You should hurry, he's summoned half the castle, I think."

Without waiting for her nod, he spun on his heel. Cassandra swallowed. She smoothed her rumpled skirts, boring gray wool, far from the lavish finery of the keep's ladies. Her belt pouch, carrying chalk and a few essential herbs, rested at her hip. She refused to enter that chamber unarmed, even if her weapons were only subtle runic lines.

The corridor leading toward the council chamber thrummed with a low, ominous hum of conversation. Pages scurried past, arms burdened with scrolls and extra chairs. Two knights flanked the double doors. Their faces gave little away, though Cassandra noticed one of them darting uneasy glances in her direction. Word traveled quickly here; no doubt they suspected the reason for Baron Ulric's abrupt summons.

She stepped inside. The broad rectangular room felt colder than usual, as though any warmth had been banished by the baron's stony gaze. At the head of a long oak table, Baron Ulric stood, knuckles pressed to the polished surface. A cluster of nobles sat arranged on either side, an uneasy mix of local lords and advisors. Their hushed murmurs fell silent the moment Cassandra appeared. She could feel their stares on her, scorn, fear, wariness, the usual.

Several seats near the far end were filled by the barony's council members, plus a handful of knights in partial armor. Taron was there, too. He stood slightly apart from everyone, posture rigid, hands folded. The tension in his frame was obvious, his shoulders so taut that the embroidered fabric of his tunic strained at the seams. Cassandra swallowed the tightness in her throat. Something was very wrong.

No one invited her to sit. She forced herself not to shrink under their scrutiny and instead moved to stand near Taron. His eyes flicked to hers, and a flicker of relief sparked there before despair took hold again.

"Cassandra…," he murmured, barely audible. "He's… about to,"

Baron Ulric raised his hand, cutting him off as he fixed on Cassandra. It felt as if the entire council chamber went still. "Now that we're all present," the baron announced, voice echoing over the hush, "it is time to address the dire threat posed by Taron's…condition." His eyes shifted toward Taron as though the word "condition" was a condemnation. "In recent weeks, we have suffered sabotage at the watchtower and farmland, all exacerbated by the uncontrollable surges of my son's magic."

A restless stir rippled among the gathered nobles. Cassandra let her gaze drift over them: some wore expressions of eager condemnation, as if they blamed Taron's volatility on her. Others looked uneasy, as if they'd prefer not to stand so close to a man whose aura might spontaneously destroy them.

Baron Ulric pressed on: "I have petitioned for a solution. We cannot proceed with these endless crises; my barony's stability is at stake."

Her heart hammered. She suspected he planned some new ultimatum, but the severity in his tone made dread coil in her chest. A glance at Taron's clenched jaw confirmed he already knew what was coming. She braced herself.

Ulric's gaze hardened. "I invoke the Rite of Desperate Measures, an ancient clause in our baronial decrees. It allows the barony to bind a witch to the noble family if her power is deemed crucial for safeguarding us from ruin, especially in a time of immediate peril."

Cassandra's blood ran cold. The Rite of Desperate Measures, she had never heard the phrase. But as Ulric's words sank in, a stifling wave of anger flared. Bind a witch. Did that mean he intended to forcibly claim her? Make her a hostage to Taron's magic without giving her the rights or respect of a noble consort?

"Sire..." The voice of an older councilman quavered from the table's far side. "Are you quite certain? Such a Rite is archaic. We have not..." He paused uncertainly. "We have not enforced it in generations."

Ulric's expression soured. "Yet it exists. It was set forth to preserve the barony from magical threats. Our predicament is dire enough, I should think. Or do we wait until Taron's next meltdown kills us all?" His words cut the air like a whip. Then, ironically calm, he continued: "Thus, I demand Taron secure a politically viable engagement in the fortnight, someone of noble standing whose alliance might strengthen the keep's hold. Otherwise, we must accept the lesser alternative." His cold gaze flicked to Cassandra, as though brandishing a weapon. "Which is to bind the witch Cassandra to our family in the barest, most expedient form, so that her warding talents remain exclusively at Taron's disposal. She would be stripped of any formal rank or protection...merely an accessory to the barony."

Fury gathered in her lungs, so sharp she could hardly breathe. He was describing her like a tool. She had endured years of exile, suspicion, sabotage, and near-death experiences trying to stabilize Taron's aura. And now Ulric was forcing an ultimatum that would see her yoked to them without rights as a recognized partner, or else Taron was to marry someone else entirely?

One of the nobles spoke up, voice trembling with a mixture of horror and fascination. "A lesser union? That is no better than...enslavement. We can't possibly,"

"Silence," Ulric snapped. "If Taron will not marry advantageously, we have no other choice. The barony's safety outweighs personal convenience."

Cassandra's fists clenched at her sides. She felt Taron's aura flicker, a faint hint of eddying magic. His shoulders shook slightly with coiled rage. She heard his shallow breathing, saw how his gaze darted to her, anguished.

She'd known Baron Ulric was oppressive, but to cast her as a lesser consort, forcibly bound to Taron's wards? As if she weren't a person but a living tool. She couldn't contain it any longer.

"This is absurd," she said, her voice slicing the hush. "You can't force me,"

"I can," Ulric interrupted, eyes narrowing. "The law is clear, if you'd bother perusing the old edicts. In the face of impending magical catastrophe, witches within the barony's domain can be compelled to serve."

A swirl of murmurs spread. Many in the room seemed scandalized, even those who disliked witches recognized the cruelty in these words. But Cassandra saw the glint in Baron Ulric's eyes, the callous inevitability he believed in. He had set the stage, and he would see it done.

Taron spoke at last, voice taut. "Father, you cannot do

this. Cassandra isn't just some unknown hedge witch, she is, she has risked her life for the keep multiple times."

Ulric's glare could have scorched the rafters. "Exactly why we need her magic firmly under our authority. You, Taron, can avoid this lesser arrangement if you promptly secure a more suitable marriage. One that will restore the faith of the local lords. A bride of respectable lineage: that is the standard remedy for a barony in crisis."

Rage coiled tighter in Cassandra's chest. She whipped her gaze around the table. "You dare treat me like...like an object? My power is my own, and I decide who to be bound to."

Her protest was drowned out by a sudden flurry of voices. Half the council spoke at once. Some cried out for caution, while others stammered that Taron's meltdown in the farmland had nearly destroyed them, and they had no choice. Cassandra felt heat pound in her veins, but a bitter chill sank in, too. Every time Taron's magic spiked, people clenched in fear. This decree from Ulric was the twisted outcome: clamp down on the source of Taron's control, Cassandra, and harness it without giving her any real standing.

Cassandra couldn't breathe. She heard one noble-woman sniff in distaste, snapping something about, "We cannot elevate a witch to ladyship first in line, nonsense. She'll sabotage Taron." Another voice hissed that forcibly binding Cassandra sounded too much like blackmail. The swirl of argument churned, making Cassandra's head spin with equal parts fury and dread.

She slammed her palm on the table. The sharp crack

silenced a few of them. Her voice rang with scorn. "Define it however you want, a lesser union is still a chain. You think you can keep me under your watch, force me to shield Taron from meltdown, without giving me the dignity of my own rights?"

Ulric's mouth curved into a thin, humorless line. "You were exiled once, Cassandra. I was under no obligation to allow you back. Do not mistake my magnanimity for weakness. This arrangement would be far more lenient than other punishments you might face should you refuse your duty.

She bristled. "Duty? You exiled me for being a witch to begin with!"

The council erupted again, and Cassandra caught Taron's voice cutting above the din: "Enough! Father, this is monstrous." His words trembled with suppressed power, as though each breath threatened to unleash a surge. "I refuse to let you reduce Cassandra to...some function, some tool to be bought or coerced."

The baron's answering snarl was immediate. "You speak as though you have a choice. Either you secure a noble bride within a fortnight, or I enact the Rite of Desperate Measures. That is final."

The chamber's tension spiked. Cassandra's chest felt tight, and she realized she was shaking. The atmosphere seemed charged with magic, Taron's aura, roiling like a caged storm. She refused to look away from Ulric's cold glare, refused to show fear.

She felt Taron shift beside her, stepping closer in a protective stance. "We are not in the Dark Ages," he said through gritted teeth. "No rational realm forcibly binds witches anymore."

Ulric just scoffed. "We do what we must so the barony does not crumble. If you care at all for these people," he waved an arm around, ", you will comply. The clock is ticking."

Cassandra's heart hammered so loudly she couldn't hear anything else for a moment. She looked at Taron, reading the anguish etched on his face. He was caught between a father who demanded compliance and a woman he clearly could not bear to see exploited. A tremor rippled through him, and faint arcs of silver light crackled around his fingertips before dissipating.

He turned back to the table and spoke again. "I will not let Cassandra be used this way," he said, voice shaking with anger. "She's not a subject to be corralled. We all stand in her debt time and time again. If I must forfeit my claim to the barony,"

"You will do no such thing!" Baron Ulric thundered, slamming his fist on the table so hard that several goblets rattled. "You are my son, and you will remain so. We have lost enough order to sabotage and rumors. I will not have you throwing your inheritance away over misguided sentiment." His gaze slashed over the room. "Is it misguided to want what's best for everyone? A stable union that cements alliances or ensures Cassandra's powers protect this keep on our terms. Enough dithering, Taron. Consider it a matter of your duty or your defiance."

At the edges of the table, some council members exchanged worried looks. Cassandra felt heat flooding her cheeks, anger and helplessness twisting into an almost unbearable knot. She glared at Ulric, who glared back, his posture laced with absolute certainty of his own authority.

Her voice trembled as she spat out, "This is an insult. I have saved Taron from meltdown after meltdown. Without me, you'd have half your farmland incinerated."

Ulric didn't flinch. "And you shall continue to do so. The question is only under what official arrangement. Now that I have made my decree, Taron, you have two options: find a noble bride, or,"

"Stop," Taron rasped, his voice trembling. "Stop acting as though Cassandra's choice doesn't matter."

Her pulse hammered in her throat. She saw how Taron's eyes pinned his father, how fury warred with heartbreak in their hazel depths. A thick silence weighed, broken only by the rustle of tapestries in an errant draft.

Finally, Ulric exhaled a scornful breath. "You will remain in this chamber until you see reason. The entire barony depends on you. If you walk away from your duty, I will hold you personally responsible for the devastation."

THIRTY-ONE

Another swirl of agitation rippled among the assembled lords, as some began clamoring for Taron to acquiesce. Cassandra's muscles tensed. She'd had enough. Enough of these people deciding her fate, ignoring her voice. Enough of them piling every burden onto Taron's shoulders while offering him no support beyond threats.

Her patience snapped. She stood straight, voice ringing: "I'm not some broodmare for your wards, Baron Ulric. I do have a say in the life forced upon me, "

Then Taron stepped into the center of the room, gaze sweeping the council. He placed a trembling hand on the table edge, expression fierce. "Father, you might brand me rebellious or ungrateful. That's fine. But I will not subject Cassandra to this lesser union, nor will I entertain parading her for the barony's convenience. If you truly desire stability, it won't be won by chaining the one person who has saved our people from sabotage more times than I can count."

A wave of uncertain murmurs. Cassandra's heart lodged somewhere in her throat. She half-expected Taron's father to fling more accusations, more threats. Indeed, Ulric's face reddened with livid anger.

"She is a witch," the baron spat, "one who nearly brought scandal upon our house before. You cannot be so blinded by,"

"Blinded?" Taron said in a shaking voice. "All I see is your obsession with control, your paranoia about my magic. Control me, control her, everything to keep your seat. You'd rather burn any compassion than risk letting me, or Cassandra, shape our own fates."

The air crackled. Cassandra sensed Taron's aura flaring, reacting to the swirl of raw emotion. She unconsciously reached for the belt pouch at her hip, feeling for her warding chalk in case she needed to anchor him. But she held back, the meltdown was not near, not yet; it was more an echo of tension.

An older noble stood abruptly, knocking his chair over. "My baron," he addressed Ulric, "the scandal would be incredible if we forcibly tethered a witch without a formal contract. People would talk. The Crown might intervene. Even if Taron tried to marry a suitable lady, the fiasco might still shake the realm."

"Silence!" Ulric roared. "Our realm is already in turmoil, thanks to Taron's surges! If not for Cassandra's wards, we'd have more farmland in ashes. It is precisely the threat of meltdown that justifies my right to bind her."

He glowered at Taron. "Surely you see we have no recourse. We're out of time."

"We are done here!" Cassandra burst out. She couldn't stand another moment of them flinging casual threats. She whirled, preparing to stride from the chamber if she had to push past blocks of disapproving nobles.

Ulric called after her, voice booming. "Where do you think you're going, witch?"

"I'm not a prisoner," she snapped. "I will not stand by and watch you parade Taron around like a pawn, and me like spare parts. Enough is enough."

She moved toward the door, ignoring glares. Her pulse pounded. Taron looked from her to his father, tension riding in every line of his body. She sensed his desperate need to protect her, to claim some shred of autonomy from this humiliating spectacle.

Ulric barked, "Taron, stay. We must settle this now, your bride's name, or the Rite is invoked."

Taron's fists tightened at his sides. He squared his shoulders, eyes alive with fury. "I told you, no. I will not do it." A hush fell, as though even the busybodies seated at the far end realized the conversation teetered on a precarious precipice. Ulric's face reddened, and for the span of several heartbeats, the baron looked fit to erupt into violence. Instead, Taron let out a shuddering breath. "I have had enough of your demands."

Ulric growled. "Damn you, Taron, I am your father and your baron. I command,"

A thunderous crack reverberated as Taron slammed his palm flat on the table. Not with magic, but with enough force to make goblets jump. "You may be my father," he said hoarsely, "but you do not have the right to do this to Cassandra, to me." Then he spun, crossing the room in swift strides. He seized Cassandra's hand, not roughly, but with urgent strength.

She let out a startled breath as he tugged her toward the door. Panicked shouts rang behind them. A swirl of motion: council members stumbling to rise, knights uncertain if they should intervene. Ulric bellowed Taron's name in raw fury. But Taron didn't look back. His gaze met Cassandra's, bright with protective anger, as he wove them between chairs and a few startled guards.

Before the watchers could rally themselves, Taron yanked open the door and pulled her out into the corridor. Their footsteps thundered on the stone floor, echoing with frantic speed. Adrenaline rushed through Cassandra, it felt both terrifying and liberating to break away from that oppressive room. Shouts reached them from behind, but none of the knights immediately pursued. Perhaps they were too shocked at the spectacle of the baron's own son defying him so openly.

They hurried along one corridor, then another. The keep's labyrinth seemed to close around them, every corner a swirl of shadow and flickering torchlight. Cassandra's pulse hammered, partly from the run, partly from the heady jumble of emotions: anger at Ulric, relief at Taron's show of solidarity, and something else hotter and more urgent. The warmth of Taron's hand around hers was impossible to ignore.

Finally, Taron tugged her into a small side hallway

near the servants' passages, a place seldom traveled by the nobility unless they were trying to avoid prying eyes. He half-collapsed against the rough stone, breathing hard, still clasping Cassandra's fingers. Torchlight wavered, throwing dancing shapes across his face.

She managed to speak between ragged breaths. "Taron... you, you just walked out. He'll...my gods, he'll punish you for that."

A shaky, humorless laugh escaped him. "I don't care," he replied, voice husky with leftover anger. "I won't let him dictate my every breath anymore. Or," He swallowed, eyes searching hers. "Or chain you like some prisoner."

She closed her eyes for a moment, head spinning. The memory of Ulric's ultimatum still seared her mind. She was furious, sick with the knowledge that the baron truly believed he could force her into such an arrangement. She fought to steady her breathing, to push back the roiling wave of helpless rage. Taron's presence next to her was an anchor, ironically enough, he felt as unsettled as she did, yet she could almost sense the swirl of magic beneath his skin. The tension of it thrummed through his clasp on her hand.

Anger bled into exasperated relief. She stared up at him, noticing the fine tremors in his shoulders. "You can't keep defying him forever," she whispered, though part of her wanted to note that she was proud, proud he hadn't cowered. "He may double down on these threats. He always does."

Taron's gaze flickered. "Let him," he nearly growled, stepping closer. The corridor's narrowness forced them to stand inches apart. Cassandra's heart lurched at the proximity. She could see the faint golden flecks in his eyes that tended to appear when his magic stirred strong. "I won't marry some noble pawn, and I won't let you," He paused, voice thick, ", be treated like that. It's vile. And I should have stopped him sooner."

Grief and a strange, fierce tenderness welled in her chest. She reached up, hesitating for an instant, then let her fingertips brush the corner of his jaw. He was trembling, but not from cold. "Taron," she murmured. "You risk everything by opposing him. Your claim, your safety, your name..."

He let out a fractured breath. "None of that matters if he destroys you in the process." A flicker of old guilt passed across his face. "I've been silent too long. When you were exiled, I let him manipulate me into standing by. I won't do it again."

She heard the raw echo of regret in his words. It was like a spark dropped onto the tinder of her carefully guarded heart, threatening to ignite. All the bitterness she'd carried warred with the knowledge that Taron was willing to tear down his father's edicts to protect her now. The swirl of emotions was dizzying.

Cassandra's chest tightened. "You know he will turn the entire keep against us," she said softly. "He'll paint me as the cause of your unrest."

Taron nodded; his breath shaky. "Then let them blame me. I'm done letting you stand alone." His hand shifted from hers to cup her elbow, then slid up toward her shoulder. His touch was warm, almost too hot, thrumming with that intangible pulse of magic. "I can't lose you," he said hoarsely. "Not to him. Not to the saboteurs."

Her heart thundered. An electric hush pooled between them. She remembered the furious council chamber, the stares, the threats, and Taron's bold refusal. The corridor felt stifling, tension coiling like a living thing. She was seething with anger at Ulric but also shaken by Taron's fierce rush to her defense. Yet deeper within, she sensed a longing she'd tried to bury for too long.

"I can stand my ground," she whispered, attempting a wry edge. "I'm no meek captive. But...thank you for not letting him steamroll me."

Taron's jaw clenched. "I only regret how long I allowed his dictates to stand. Cassandra, I,"

She sighed, letting her fingertips slide from his jaw to the back of his neck. The contact ignited sparks along her nerves. "I know," she murmured. "You were caught, too."

He exhaled, and his next words came in a hollow rush: "I'm sorry. Sorry for everything, for letting him do this, for my complicity in your exile, for the way the barony keeps seeing you as a tool, despite your sacrifices." His eyes shone with raw sincerity. "I know you can defend yourself, but... I also know you shouldn't have to do it alone. Not this time."

THIRTY-TWO

Her pulse stuttered, tears biting at the back of her eyes. She would not cry, not here, not now. Her voice shook with the thickness of suppressed feeling. "You realize that if we stand against him together, we have no guarantee. He's threatened to basically enslave me in this lesser union. He's threatened to force you into a marriage. Taron...there's no easy fix."

A faint trace of a sad smile curled Taron's lips. "Then we'll walk this path together, no matter how precarious. I can't sacrifice you for a convenient alliance. I refused once in that chamber, and I'll keep refusing." His voice dropped, taking on a low, urgent intensity. "I have never wanted anything more than to protect you, Cassandra."

Her breath caught. The corridor's torch flickered, revealing the faint lines of exhaustion around Taron's eyes. He was terrified, she realized. Terrified of losing control of his magic, losing her, losing what vestiges of respect he still had among the barony's ranks. But at that moment, the fear only fed the blazing determination in him.

She parted her lips to speak, but the words tangled on her tongue. Her anger at Ulric mingled with fierce gratitude, for Taron's stand, for the unguarded yearning in his eyes now. She could practically feel the air crackling around them, heavy with unspoken confessions. Time felt suspended.

Then Taron moved. He slid his arm around her waist, pulling her against him in a single, swift motion. She gasped softly, but it wasn't fear that stuttered through her. It was longing, an echo of the closeness they once had, sharpened by everything that had gone wrong between them. Heat flared in her cheeks, and she saw that same heat reflected in Taron's expression.

She didn't resist. Perhaps she should have, but her heart hammered too loudly for logic to keep pace. Anger and desire coalesced, fueling an undeniable pull. The swirl of frustration, defiance, and lingering heartbreak found an outlet in the desperate need to feel something real, something that wasn't the baron's manipulations or the conspirators' sabotage.

His voice shuddered. "I will find a way out of this, some path that spares you from father's ultimatum. I swear it."

She laid a trembling palm against his chest, feeling the thud of his racing heartbeat beneath the embroidered fabric. "I'm, I'm not going to run anymore," she whispered. "Not from you, not from this barony, no matter how they brand me. But Taron...we must be careful." She wasn't sure if she meant the political ramifications or the precariousness of the magic simmering beneath his skin.

A tight nod. "Yes," he agreed softly, though caution seemed far from his mind. In the dim corridor, with distant voices still echoing from the council chamber behind them, Taron's gaze locked on Cassandra's. He bent his head, drawing closer. Her heart jolted, and she found herself tilting her face up, lips parting in unspoken invitation.

Then that tension snapped. Taron lowered his mouth to hers in an urgent, desperate kiss. She pressed back, the taste of his breath as heady as any enchantment. She realized tears were stinging her eyes, tears of anger at Ulric's cruelty, at lost years, at the relief of not being alone in this fight anymore.

The corridor's shadows seemed to expand, wrapping them in heated darkness. Their surroundings blurred as Taron led her—kissing all the way—into a hidden alcove behind thick drapes. The only immediate reality was the press of Taron's body, the tangle of her fingers in his hair, the raw drive of him needing to prove, through touch and closeness, that they were more than pawns in a baron's game.

He drew back for a single second, panting, eyes bright with a swirl of longing and near-despair. "Cassandra," he breathed, voice cracking, "please...tell me I haven't ruined everything."

Fresh anger at Ulric welled. Maybe Taron had once let her down, but now, faced with a father's ultimatum that threatened them both, he was choosing a different path.

She shook her head, pressing her forehead to his. "You haven't," she whispered, taking a shuddery breath. "We may have no idea how to fix this, but you haven't lost me."

He closed his eyes, relief crossing his features. Then he kissed her again. His hands, strong and sure, slid to her waist, the warmth of his palms searing through the layers of her tunic. He pulled her closer until there was no space between them, the hard planes of his body pressing into hers, grounding her even as the world felt as though it were spinning out of control.

Cassandra gasped against his mouth, her fingers tangling in the soft strands of his dark hair, and Taron groaned softly in response, the sound rumbling through her and igniting every nerve in her body. His lips left hers, trailing down her jawline to the curve of her neck, where his breath burned hot against her skin. She tilted her head instinctively, granting him better access, and he didn't hesitate. The soft scrape of his stubble against her throat sent a shiver down her spine, her pulse racing as his kisses grew more fervent, more consuming.

Her hands slid down his chest, fingers brushing over the embroidery of his tunic before finding the fastenings. She tugged, and Taron stilled briefly, his forehead resting against hers, their breath mingling in the heated space between them. His voice was hoarse, almost reverent. "Cassandra... Are you sure?"

Her chest heaved, her heart pounding so loudly she could barely hear her own reply. "I'm sure. I've never been more sure." Her fingers trembled slightly as she worked the fastenings free, exposing the warm, hard muscle beneath. Taron exhaled a shuddering breath, his hands moving to her back, tracing the curve of her spine through the fabric before gripping the edges of her tunic.

He lifted it over her head in one swift motion, the cool air of the corridor brushing her bare skin before his hands returned, calloused and gentle as they explored her shoulders and arms. The sensation sent a wave of heat rushing through her, and she stepped closer, her own hands finding the bare skin of his chest. His aura, always a faint hum around him, seemed to spark at her touch, the golden glow flaring faintly in the dim light.

"Taron," she whispered, her voice catching as his hands slid to her waist, then lower, gripping her hips and lifting her against him. He pressed her back against the rough stone wall, the contrast of its cool surface and his fiery touch making her gasp. His lips found hers again, more demanding this time, and she met him with equal fervor, her legs wrapping around his waist as he held her there with ease.

Magic crackled in the air around them, faint tendrils of gold and blue light swirling like embers caught in the wind. Cassandra felt the heat of it against her skin, but it wasn't chaotic or dangerous. It was controlled, focused, as though their connection had steadied the storm inside him. Taron's lips left hers, trailing down her neck and across her collarbone, his hands sliding under her thighs to grip her firmly. Every touch, every kiss sent waves of pleasure coursing through her, building with an intensity that made her head spin.

She arched against him, her fingers digging into his

shoulders as his mouth continued its path lower, and the faint flicker of light from his aura seemed to pulse in time with her racing heartbeat. Taron's breath hitched, his hands tightening on her as he paused, his forehead pressing against her shoulder. "You... calm it," he murmured, his voice thick with emotion. "The storm... it's quiet when I'm with you."

Her heart clenched at his words, and she cupped his face, forcing him to meet her gaze. His eyes glowed faintly, the golden flecks shimmering in the dim light, but they were steady—no longer wild or afraid. "We calm each other," she whispered, brushing her thumb over his cheekbone. "Whatever chaos there is, we'll face it together."

Taron's expression softened, his hands moving to cradle her face as though she were the most precious thing in the world. "Cassandra," he said, her name a reverent prayer on his lips, before he kissed her again, slower this time, savoring every second. His magic flared once more, wrapping around them like a cocoon of warmth and light, and she felt its pulse settle, steady and sure, as their bodies moved in perfect harmony.

When the tension between them finally broke, it did so in a wave of release that left them both trembling, their breaths mingling in the stillness that followed. Taron held her close, his forehead resting against hers, and she felt the faint glow of his magic retreat, quiet and controlled. His hands stroked her back in lazy circles, and she felt her own magic settle in response, the storm in both of them replaced by a profound calm.

"You were right," he murmured after a moment, his voice soft but certain. "We do calm each other. You're my balance, Cassandra."

Her chest tightened, and she pressed a gentle kiss to his lips. "And you're mine." She let her head rest against his shoulder, their bodies still entwined as the corridor's shadows seemed to hold them in their own private world.

Far down the corridor, footsteps pounded toward them. A voice called, "Lord Taron! Where are--" then there was a startled cutoff. breath ragged. He peeked through the drapes then turned back to her. He exhaled as they both dressed. "We can't let them see us like this."

Her heart still hammered, lips feeling swollen from that fierce exchange. "Then we find somewhere more discreet," she said. Warmth burned through her cheeks at her own boldness.

With a curt nod, Taron suddenly grabbed her hand again, leading her away from the corridor. They passed a startled page who quickly ducked aside, no doubt taking note of Taron's disheveled hair and Cassandra's breathless flush. But Taron didn't slow. He guided her down a short flight of steps into an even narrower side passage, seldom used except by servants. The flickering sconces were spaced out, leaving pockets of near-darkness.

Halfway down this passage, Taron paused by a small recess in the wall. A dusty tapestry hung overhead, hiding a battered door behind it. He nudged the tapestry aside, then pushed the door open just enough to slip through, pulling Cassandra with him. The cramped space beyond was barely big enough for two people standing close, likely an unused storage alcove for cleaning brushes or old linens. But it was private, and the hush swallowed them almost immediately.

She leaned against the rough stone, breath quick. Taron let the door shut behind them. Darkness enfolded them except for the faint glow seeping through cracks around the doorframe. In that gloom, her senses sharpened: the scent of his skin, the faint dust in the air, the pounding of both their hearts.

He pressed closer, hands braced on either side of her as if to cage her in, though the tension in his posture was anything but predatory. It was protective, anguished, and, above all, fervent. "I can't bear that he wants to treat you like property," Taron rasped. "You deserve so much more."

She swallowed, her hands lifting to rest on his chest. His heart hammered under her palms. "I appreciate that." A small, shaky laugh escaped her. "Though for the record, I'd never let him do it without a fight. Nor will I let you sacrifice yourself in the process."

He nodded, forehead lowering to brush hers. "We'll stand together. We'll figure out how to stop him, how to reveal the sabotage, all of it." A haunted glimmer passed through his eyes. "You make me feel...like there's hope beyond father's cruelty. That I could still fix the damage."

Emotions tumbled within her. She didn't respond with words, only reached up to clasp the back of his neck, pulling him into another hungry kiss. This time, there was no lingering uncertainty. She parted her lips, letting him taste the depth of her frustration and want. He answered in kind, a low sound vibrating in his throat as he cupped her cheek with one hand. The press of his body against hers radiated a heat that sank down to her bones, banishing the chill that had followed them all morning.

Her own anger flared again, anger at Ulric, at the sabotage, at the keep's endless hostility. But here, in the dark of this hidden alcove, anger transformed into a potent, defiant passion. She poured every unspoken feeling into that kiss, her resentment of the baron's manipulations, her longing for Taron that neither time nor betrayal had snuffed out. It felt as though they stood at the edge of a precipice, about to leap together, uncertain of the future but certain they could not step back.

Cassandra's breath turned shallow. Taron's magic flickered faintly, tingling across her skin like static, though she felt no fear. She rested a hand on his forearm, silently grounding him. He responded by sliding a hand around her waist, beneath the fall of her cloak, fingers splayed out with unbridled hunger. Their bodies pressed more tightly together, his heartbeat pounding in time with her own.

She barely recognized her own voice, husky and breathless. "Taron…" The single word carried a hundred entangled emotions: fury, need, promise, dread. She wanted to devour him, to cling to him, to relinquish every burden for a moment of raw human connection.

He answered by capturing her mouth again, almost reverent this time. Their surroundings blurred as he surrendered to that kiss with a desperation that made her chest ache. She could feel the stone at her back, feel the slight scratch of his tunic's embroidery against her arms, feel the mingled swirl of their breath. Reality narrowed to this cramped hiding spot, to the taste and feel of him, to the thunderous knowledge that they were forging their own path, one that defied Ulric's decree and the entire council's condemnation.

Between their panting gasps, Taron finally tore his lips away, only to bury his face against her neck. "I can't lose you," he repeated brokenly. His voice sounded thick, as though the weight of the barony's expectations crushed him. "I won't,"

"Hush," she murmured, threading her fingers through his hair, letting him rest there a moment. "We won't let him tear us apart." Inside, she still trembled at the enormity of the baron's threat, but right now, this closeness, this unity, was the only solace she had.

He lifted his head again, gaze full of raw honesty. "Cassandra, I,"

She silenced him with another kiss, gentler this time but no less charged. A burning wave of need surged, and she let it guide her as she pressed her body flush to his, arms tightening around his neck. This moment was a refuge from the raging storm outside. Yes, they would have to face the baron again. Yes, they needed a plan to dismantle the sabotage. But for now...

Her lips parted, and Taron groaned softly, reciprocating with a fierceness that left her blood humming. He angled his head, deepening their connection, one hand slipping beneath the edge of her bodice while the other braced on the wall behind her. She curled her fingers in his hair, that faint crackle of magic dancing along her skin again, pulsing in time with her racing pulse.

They broke apart only for air, and Taron's eyes shone in the dimness. His voice trembled with intensity. "Cassandra, we can't stay here...someone'll find us." Yet even as he said it, he dipped his head to nip gently at her jaw, pulling a low gasp from her throat.

She coughed a strained laugh, breathless. "Do you really care right now?"

He gave a short, almost desperate groan. "Only that I can't stand the thought of your name on their tongues if they catch us. And, I want," He struggled for composure. "I need you without every prying eye and these damned stone walls, but..." His gaze flicked to the rickety door behind them. "At least we have a little privacy here."

Her heart pounded with agreement. She pressed her forehead to his, letting her eyes close as she inhaled. "We shouldn't linger," she whispered. "But just, just a moment more."

He captured her lips again, and the world tilted. The kiss turned heated, mouths parting with mounting hunger. She fumbled at the collar of his tunic, wanting to abandon reason to the rush of closeness. Every nerve felt alive, as though his aura lured her deeper into an intimacy that neither of them had allowed themselves to fully embrace until this crisis drew them together.

His hand slid along her waist, then up the back of her neck, tangling in her hair. She exhaled a broken sound, letting her arms come up around his shoulders. The tension that had battered them in the council chamber transmuted into raw, unrestrained need. She realized with a surge of wonder that, despite all the near meltdowns and conspiracies, Taron's presence felt like home.

Outside, muffled footsteps passed, but no one tried the door. Cassandra hardly noticed. The press of Taron's body, the ragged exhalations of breath, the scalding kisses, these sensations consumed her. She welcomed it, letting the flood of desire drown out the baron's threats for one precious moment.

Finally, as if by mutual, unspoken agreement, that mounting urgency swelled to a breaking point. Their kisses turned frenzied, hands roaming, lips trailing down throats, breath catching in small moans. Taron pressed her firmly against the wall, and the rising heat of his magic seemed to swirl around them, not in danger but in heightened awareness. She was vaguely aware of how daring it was, how the barony might label her a scandalous temptress, but she didn't care. All that mattered was that Taron wanted her, that he was choosing her, that he risked everything for her, and she for him.

His gaze locked onto her, a silent question shining in his eyes. Cassandra answered by sliding her hand down to his belt, meeting his mouth once more. The air tasted of dust, tension, and an undercurrent of unstoppable yearning. They kissed again, deeper, more purposefully. The rest of the keep's turmoil melted away, leaving only this potent, fiercely private moment. They poured unspoken confessions into every caress, apologies for the past, oaths for the future, raw desire for the present.

Cassandra felt the prickle of tears again at the corners of her eyes. She let them go, let them mingle with the urgency of Taron's lips. Deep inside, she felt a spark of defiance: let the baron scowl and the council gossip. They could not smother the truth of what Taron and Cassandra shared. His father could enforce edicts, sabotage could threaten their lives, but here, in the hush of this hidden alcove, they reclaimed a piece of themselves that had been denied for too long.

As Taron's mouth trailed hotly against her jaw and down her throat, she arched into him, a soft cry escaping. His hand slipped beneath her cloak, seeking the heat of her skin, guiding her deeper against his chest. Adrenaline rushed like a river in her veins. She felt that molten, desperate swirl cresting, a vow unspoken on her lips.

Their kisses turned desperate, teeth and tongues meeting in a frenzied dance. The corridor outside must still be alive with debate, searching knights, scandalized council members, but they were lost to it now, the pounding of their hearts and the friction of heated breaths overwhelming all else. Their defiance and need, stoked higher by the baron's ultimatum, fueled each feverish touch.

"I won't let him hurt you," Taron gasped against her lips, voice trembling. "Never again." And in that promise, Cassandra heard everything he had failed to do before, and everything he hoped to do now.

She answered with a breathless vow of her own, though words failed her. Instead, she slid her arms around his neck and captured his mouth yet again. The rest of the world vanished in that fiery union of frustration and longing. They pressed together in the cramped darkness, surrendering to the volcanic tide of desire that had pulsed beneath all their tensions and confessions for so long.

Neither knew who moved first, but in the next heartbeat, Taron gently eased her toward the far corner of the alcove, away from any stray eyes that might peep through the door's crack. His lips found hers again, hungry and soft in equal measure, and Cassandra answered with a fervor that jolted through her entire body. The rickety door thumped shut behind them more soundly, sealing them in absolute secrecy. Her cloak rustled, his hands traveling over her curves, and she responded in kind, letting her fingers roam the planes of his torso, the lines of his shoulders.

With a trembling exhale, Taron pressed his cheek against hers, letting out a soft, urgent moan. The tension between them burned so fiercely that Cassandra's mind spun. For a moment, she let the swirl of magic and adrenaline carry her away, away from sabotage, from the baron's hateful decree. She clutched at Taron, meeting his gaze in the dimness, seeing every ounce of his devotion and fear laid bare.

He dove forward again, capturing her lips, this time with gentleness that melted her bones. In that kiss, she felt the unspoken truths bridging the chasms left by old betrayals, forging a new bond beyond the baron's control. They lost themselves in each other, the hush wrapping them in a cocoon of unbridled longing. Heartbeats thundered, hands fumbled at the edges of clothing, and the alcove was filled with ragged whispers of desperation, promises, and love unspoken but present in every breath.

Neither heard the muted clamor of footsteps in the hall, nor did they care. Together, they sank into that tide, releasing fear, letting anger transform into the fierce heat of a connection long overdue. When at last they broke for air, Taron's eyes gleamed with unshed tears, and Cassandra's pulse hammered in her ears.

Outside, the keep might riot with gossip. The baron might twist the law. The next battles would be fierce. But in this stolen alcove, in the lingering hush, Taron and Cassandra surrendered to the promise that had ignited between them years ago, now stoked to blazing life by desperation and defiance.

Their breathing ragged, Taron brushed his lips against her temple. "I want you," he whispered, his voice cracking with emotion. "All of you."

Her reply was only a trembling kiss, as she pulled him closer, letting him feel the intensity of her answer. No council edict, no forced vow, no sabotage could overshadow what bound them in this moment. Against the old stone, under the hush of near-darkness, they kindled a fierce vow of their own.

THE STORY CONTINUES

The Story Continues in book three, *Seduction,* coming soon to Amazon.

EXCERPT FROM BOOK THREE: SEDUCTION

CHAPTER ONE

Cassandra woke before dawn. Despite exhaustion tugging at every muscle, her heart still hammered from the stolen intimate moments from the night before when she and Taron were in the secluded alcove. The taste of his lips, the hush of his breath against her cheek, this was all she'd allowed herself to recall since slipping away hours ago. The keep lay in near silence now, but she sensed tension in the corridors as if the stones themselves harbored secrets.

She pushed back the thin blanket and swung her legs over the side of her narrow bed. Her mind churned with emotions, swirling between worry and a traitorous spark of happiness. No matter how she tried to guard herself against it, Taron's touch reverberated through her. She'd built her emotional walls high, but last night they'd crumbled in a cascade of longing, anger, and shared need.

But the aftermath of their lovemaking could be devastating. Baron Ulric, Taron's father, would never tolerate them openly seeking comfort in each other's arms, and to make matters worse they'd left the council chamber in a storm. Taron had defied his father so fiercely that the entire keep must still be buzzing with rumors about what had happened and was coming next. And Cassandra, her cheeks warmed at the memory, recalling how recklessly she'd clung to Taron, how his kisses had stumblingly melted her anger into pure flame.

Now, though, everything felt too heavy. An eerie thrum prickled at the edge of her senses; the aura of wards disturbed her. Taron's wards, she thought immediately, pulse kicking up. She rose from the bed, ignoring the stiffness in her limbs, and tugged on a cloak over her rumpled shift. Shielding a candle's flame with one hand, she slipped into the dim hallway.

The corridor was only faintly lit, a single torch sputtering in its bracket. Shadows danced across the stones. As Cassandra ventured out, the hairs on her arms rose. She paused near a bend in the hallway, then pressed her palm flat to the wall, feeling for the faintest trace of runic lines. She caught just a whisper of something sinister, runic symbols, but not those used for healing or harmless illusions. These felt sharper, menacing.

Danger. It flared through her bones like a warning bell. She quickened her pace in the direction of Taron's chambers. A low lamp flickered near the heavy wooden door that led to his suite. The guard normally stationed there was nowhere to be seen; instead, the space looked deserted. Her pulse soared.

"Taron?" she called softly. No response echoed back.

She reached the threshold and halted. The candlelight

from her hand revealed spidery lines etched on the stone floor just outside Taron's door, dark, twisted runes arranged in a branching pattern. Unease constricted her chest. She crouched down, letting the candlelight spill across the imprints. The lines were definitely fresh, the chalk residue lying in faint smears that indicated hurried work.

Cursed runes, she realized grimly. They were designed to latch onto Taron's aura and pull it out of balance, inciting an explosive surge. She'd heard rumors of such sabotage but had never seen them so blatantly placed, so near Taron's chamber. Her heartbeat thudded. If Taron stirred inside or if his magic flared on its own, these runes could trigger a catastrophic blast, possibly leveling half this hall, and damning Taron.

She pressed a hand against the cold stone, reaching out with her own wards. Instantly, the runic pattern seethed, pricking her senses with malicious power. She swore under her breath. This was no trivial hex. The saboteur intended to detonate Taron's surges while he slept or at least catch him off guard.

Biting back fear, she set her candle aside and dug into the belt pouch at her waist, she always carried a few scraps of chalk, a small vial of warding oil. The sabotage had to be nullified, but the risk was immense. A single miscalculation, and the runes might detonate.

"All right," she whispered, throat tight. "Steady."

She took out a piece of chalk and hastily drew three more symbols onto the floor. The first stroke of her chalk flared with pale luminescence. She grimaced; that reaction meant the sabotage runes were pulsing with energy, readying themselves for activation. Possibly keyed to Taron's presence, or to the next time he lost even a fraction of control.

"Not now," she muttered, working quicker. Chalk dust smeared her fingertips as she drew a rough circle around the three sigils. She had to isolate these runes from Taron's aura, bind them together to apply a barrier strong enough to keep them from igniting. Nights spent training in the forest with Miriana had taught her that cursed runes always tried to bite back, like cornered predators.

Cassandra coaxed a thin thread of her own magic onto the floor, weaving it in a slow arc around the symbols meant to sabotage their enemies. She felt the runes snapping at her wards, each intersection sizzling with dark sparks. Her heart pounded as she forced them back, bit by bit. Not only did she have to contain them, but she also had to neutralize their link.

The original runes hissed like a kettle about to boil, steam rising from the stone upon which they were drawn. For a heartbeat, she felt them tugging at Taron's aura, as though searching for him. She pictured Taron in his chamber, perhaps fitfully asleep, and the idea that these cursed runes might drain him or force a meltdown left her furious and terrified in equal measure. She poured more energy into her wards, sweat beading at her temple.

A sudden crackle split the silence. Cassandra's circle wavered. The runes swelled with a sickly green glow, sending a jolt up her arm. A cry ripped from her throat; agony lanced her nerves. She fought to keep her chalk pressed to the stone, continuing the final lines of the containment circle. If she stopped now, it'd be worse.

She completed the last symbol with a shaky flourish. The chalk lines flared bright, and the cursed runes flickered. She felt them recoil, locked within the circle, but they didn't vanish. Their malicious presence seethed like caged thunder. Cassandra's arms trembled.

She needed to strengthen the hold, disentangle the sabotage's anchor to Taron. That required a second loop of runes, a layered approach. She swallowed the knot of worry. With one hand still pressed to her circle, she tried to rummage for the small bottle of warding oil.

Her vision swam. The dark runes fought against her magic, draining more from her than she expected. She grit her teeth, pushing back. "You won't...win," she rasped, blinking away black spots.

The sabotage flared again, a silent ripple that made the hallway lantern flicker. Cassandra's circle cracked in places. She sketched frantic repairs, each movement of her chalk precise but unsteady.

"Cassandra!"

Her head jerked up to see Taron sprinting from around the corner. She hadn't realized how dazed she was until relief swelled in her chest. His hair was tousled, and he wore only breeches and a partly unbuttoned tunic, as though he'd thrown clothes on in a rush. How he'd known, she didn't care. She was just grateful to see him.

"Stay back!" she shouted, voice trembling. "There are cursed runes."

He skidded to a halt a few paces away, eyes widening

at the pale greenish light shimmering on the floor. "Gods," he breathed. "Are you—?"

She shook her head vigorously to cut him off. "I've locked them in a containment circle, but it's not stable. If you get too close with your aura...they'll feed on it."

Taron's face darkened. "I felt the pull from down the hall, like something yanking at my core. I had to come."

Cassandra clenched her teeth. Another surge from the sabotage lines buckled her half-drawn wards. Pain speared through her, and she dropped to one knee. "They're trying to force your magic out," she gasped, voice tight. "I can't let them--"

Before she could finish, a violent jolt coursed through the runes, lighting the corridor in a flash of sickly green. Cassandra cried out, arms shaking as she fought to maintain the circle. She felt her stamina draining fast.

Taron started forward. "I'll help,"

"No!" she snapped, flinching as the sabotage lines hissed. "If you come closer, they'll latch onto you. I have to sever their anchor first."

His jaw set with fierce determination. He shot a glance behind him, presumably checking if any guards had heard the commotion, but the corridor remained eerily empty. Cassandra's vision blurred, and the floor pooled with sweat from her brow. She swallowed hard, ignoring the pounding of her skull.

Focus. Just a little more. She forced an unsteady exhale, raising her warding chalk to inscribe a second series of runes around the first. Each stroke took monumental effort. Fiery threads of her magic poured forth, weaving a ring of pale gold that contended with the sabotage's noxious hue. She felt Taron's presence like a beacon, his aura trembling at the edge of her senses, full of alarm but forced to remain still lest he provoke a meltdown.

The sabotage lines snapped, spitting sparks that scorched the stone. Cassandra swore under her breath as a jolt nearly tore the chalk from her fist. She blinked away tears. Another wave of draining heat slammed her, making her entire body tremble.

OTHER FLORID ROMANCE BOOKS

To be notified of new releases and special promotions from Florid Romance, please join our email list:

https://floridromance.lmbpn.com/about/sign-up-for-our-newsletter/

For a complete list of books published by Florid Romance please visit our website:

https://floridromance.lmbpn.com/

BOOKS BY RIVER TATUM

The Dating Diary
One Is Too Many BF's (Book 1)
Two Many Choices (Book 2)
Three is A Crowd (Book 3)
Four Is a Disaster (Book 4)

The Firebrand Chronicles
Forged in Flame (Book 1)
Bound By Flame and Illusion (Book 2)
Crowned in Flame and Oath (Book 3)

Vows in Magic and Steel
Duty Bound (Book 1)
Hearts in Conflict (Book 2)
Unbreakable Vows (Book 3)

Sorcery and Secrets

Sabotage (Book 1)
Suspicion (Book 2)
Seduction (Book 3)

BOOKS BY MICHAEL ANDERLE

CONNECT WITH MICHAEL ANDERLE

Connect with Michael Anderle

Website: http://lmbpn.com

Email List: https://michael.beehiiv.com/

https://www.facebook.com/LMBPNPublishing

https://twitter.com/MichaelAnderle

https://www.instagram.com/lmbpn_publishing/

https://www.bookbub.com/authors/michael-anderle